DARK DAYS

Join Ωmega today!

DARK DAYS

JAMES PONTI

ALADDIN

NEW YORK LONDON TORONTO SYDNEY NEW DELHI

For Fiona,
who heard Molly's voice right from the start

ALADDIN

An imprint of Simon & Schuster Children's Publishing Division
1230 Avenue of the Americas, New York, New York 10020
First Aladdin paperback edition October 2016
Text copyright © 2015 by James Ponti
Cover illustration copyright © 2015 by Nigel Quarless
Also available in an Aladdin hardcover edition.

ALADDIN is a trademark of Simon & Schuster, Inc., and related logo is a registered trademark of Simon & Schuster, Inc.
For information about special discounts for bulk purchases, please contact Simon & Schuster Special Sales at 1-866-506-1949 or business@simonandschuster.com.
The Simon & Schuster Speakers Bureau can bring authors to your live event. For more information or to book an event contact the Simon & Schuster Speakers Bureau at 1-866-248-3049 or visit our website at www.simonspeakers.com.
Series designed by Lisa Vega
Jacket designed by Jessica Handelman
The text of this book was set in Adobe Garamond Pro.
Manufactured in the United States of America 0816 OFF
10 9 8 7 6 5 4 3 2 1
The Library of Congress has cataloged the hardcover edition as follows:
Ponti, James.
Dark days / by James Ponti.—First Aladdin hardcover edition.
pages cm.—(Dead City; book 3)
Summary: "Molly Bigelow and her Omega team have been banned from investigating Marek Blackwell and his plans for New York City. But when they discover that Blackwell is raising money for a zombie army, they have to act. But will they be in time?"—Provided by publisher.
ISBN 978-1-4814-3636-6 (hc)
[1. Zombies—Fiction. 2. Supernatural—Fiction. 3. Secret societies—Fiction. 4. New York (N.Y.)—Fiction.] I. Title.
PZ7.P7726Dar 2015
[Fic]—dc23
2014046622
ISBN 978-1-4814-3637-3 (pbk)
ISBN 978-1-4814-3638-0 (eBook)

You're probably wondering what I'm doing in jail…

My dad says you should always look on the bright side of things, and normally that's great advice. Like when I had to have my tonsils out, but I also got to eat as much ice cream as I wanted. Or when our weekend on the Jersey shore got canceled, but we ended up going to a Yankees–Red Sox game instead.

I was even able to find a bright side on the first day of school when a maniac zombie attacked me in the Roosevelt Island subway station. (It led to a group of amazing friends and a secret life watching over the world of the undead.) But lately the bright sides in my life have been harder to find.

I mean, what's good about the evil lord of the zombies—you know the one I was totally sure I helped kill—surprising everyone by reappearing even more powerful than ever? Or how about Omega, the secret society I'm a member of, the one that's responsible for maintaining the balance of power and peace between the living and the undead, having to suspend all activity because our security has broken down and the lives of everyone I care about have been endangered?

Then there's my current situation.

Right now I'm sitting on a bench in the middle of Central Park, which sounds kind of bright side-y until you realize the bench is in a holding cell in the Central Park precinct of the New York Police Department.

That's right. I, Molly Bigelow, Little Miss Goody-Two shoes who's never gotten so much as an after-school detention, am in jail. If you can think of anything positive about this, I'd love to hear it; because when my dad gets here, I'm pretty sure he's going to focus on the *getting arrested* part.

I can already hear the conversation: *Gee, Molly, when you said you were going to the Central Park Zoo, I assumed the animals would be the only ones behind bars. You're grounded for life!*

I was charged with disturbing the peace because I jumped

into the water at the sea lion exhibit. I did it in a moment of desperation, and while it seemed like a good idea at the time, I now realize it was a flawed plan.

First of all, the water was way colder than I expected. I'm talking like-a-brain-freeze-but-all-over-your-body cold. And secondly, I didn't think about the fact that I'd be stuck in wet clothes for the rest of the day. Being arrested is bad enough, but being arrested in waterlogged jeans, wet underwear, and sneakers that squish every time you take a step is even worse.

The officer who arrested me was actually pretty nice about it. Her name is Strickland, and instead of putting me in handcuffs, she just led me to her squad car, no doubt confident that if I made a run for it she could easily track me down by following the wet shoe prints.

Once we got to the precinct I was fingerprinted and had my mug shots taken. (By the way, remind me not to jump fully clothed into a pool right before next year's yearbook pictures. The wet look and I are not a good match.) Next I got to use my one phone call to let my father know where I was. That was pleasant. I'll skip the specifics, but the conversation quickly went from "Are you all right?" to *"Are you insane?"* Then I put him on with Officer Strickland.

They talked for a minute or two, and at one point she

even laughed. Afterward she told me that she had some good news and some bad news. The good was that once my father arrived I was going to be released with a warning.

"Although," she added, "if you ever want to go back to the Central Park Zoo, you owe them about fifty hours of volunteer work."

"I guess that's fair," I replied.

"It will probably involve a shovel and animal poop."

The thought of that made me cringe. "Is the animal poop the bad news?"

"No," she laughed. "That's still part of the good. The bad news is that your dad can't pick you up until his shift is over, so you're going to have to spend a few hours in the holding cell."

That's where I am right now, sitting on a wooden bench in the holding cell with a small puddle of water around my feet. The cell is about twice the size of my bedroom, and, for the moment at least, I'm alone. I guess that's technically a bright side; but I think when the bright side is that your jail situation could be worse, then things are still pretty bad.

So why did I do it? Why did I climb up on the rail and cannonball into the freezing water? Was I escaping a crazed zombie? Was I protesting the treatment of animals held in captivity? Was I just being . . . *stupid*?

No, no, and no. Although, the stupid one is debatable. The truth is that I was *trying* to get arrested, and not just anywhere. I needed to get arrested in Central Park so that I would wind up in this precinct, in this holding cell. In that sense I was successful. I just should have figured out how to get here without the wet underwear. (And without the whole shoveling of animal poop thing.)

If the rest of my plan works—and judging by my recent success rate, that's iffy at best—things are going to get a little crazy before I walk out of here. (Actually, if the plan works I won't be *walking* out, but I'll save that part of the story for later.) And if it doesn't work, well, then I'll have a lot of explaining to do when my father arrives. Either way, I'm not going anywhere for a while, so I might as well try to explain how it all happened. Who knows, maybe I'll notice something I missed the first time around. Something that will help me pull this off, because if I don't, New York might have front row seats for the zombie apocalypse.

It all started just a few blocks from here on a January morning when I was too stubborn to come in out of the snow. . . .

The Hamlet Suite

The biggest lie perpetrated by the Christmas card industry has nothing to do with flying reindeer and everything to do with snow. Greeting card snow is festive and fun, but real snow is just cold and annoying. That's why all the people on the sidewalk were hurrying to get out of it. Well, all of them except for me.

"You know we could always wait inside," Grayson said, pointing toward the lobby with his head so he didn't have to take his hands out of his pockets. "I hear they've got electricity and heat."

"If we go in the lobby, Hector will send us up to the

apartment; and I don't want to go to the apartment without Alex," I replied. "I want us all to go together. Like a team."

Hector was the doorman in Natalie's building, and like all good doormen on the Upper West Side he didn't let you just hang out in his lobby. He kept you moving, especially when the weather was bad. That meant we had two options: stand in the snow and wait for Alex, or go up to Natalie's apartment and start without him.

"Let's just give him five more minutes," I said. "If he isn't here by then, we'll go anyway."

It was the first time we were visiting Natalie since she'd been released from the hospital. The first time the four of us were going to be alone since the epic failure that was New Year's Eve, when Marek Blackwell came back from the dead and Natalie wound up in intensive care.

Even though I was excited to see her, a part of me was dreading it. I felt responsible for everything that happened and wouldn't have been surprised if she blamed me too. I was worried that our friendship, which meant everything to me, was about to come to a sudden end. That's why I wanted to wait for Alex. I needed all the friendly faces I could get.

"Is everything all right?"

A police officer was asking us. He was tall, over six feet,

and had broad shoulders. His name tag said PELL and he was curious as to why Grayson and I didn't have enough sense to get out of the snow.

"We're fine, officer," I replied. "We're just waiting for a friend."

"Well, don't wait too long or you'll catch cold," he said. "Or even worse, your ears might freeze off."

"That would be bad," I said with a laugh. "I like my ears right where they are."

He gave me a strange look and replied with sudden seriousness, "I'm not joking. Do you have any idea what that looks like?"

I traded a bewildered glance with Grayson before I asked, "Do I have any idea what what looks like?"

"What it looks like when your ears freeze off?" he said. "It's terrible. Let me show you."

With no further warning, Officer Pell reached up and peeled his left ear off the side of his head. A pulpy green membrane hung from it as he dangled it in front of my face and started laughing. That's when I noticed his orange and yellow teeth and realized that in addition to being one of New York's Finest, he was also one of New York's Deadest. He was a Level 2 zombie with a twisted sense of humor.

I let out a scream and that only made him laugh harder.

Between the snow, the traffic, and everybody rushing along the sidewalk, no one even noticed. You gotta love New York.

"Let this be a warning," he said as he waved it by the lobe, pieces of zombie ear goop flinging past our faces. "We've got our eyes on you."

He thought for a second and chuckled before adding, "And now I guess . . . we've got our ears on you too." With that, he flicked the ear right at me and it stuck to my jacket.

I did a hand flap dance for a couple seconds until I knocked it off, and by the time the ear hit the ground, Officer Pell had disappeared into the crowd.

Grayson stared at me in stunned silence before stammering, "Did that really just happen? Did that really just happen?"

I nodded rather than answer, worried that if I opened my mouth my lunch might spew all over the sidewalk.

The encounter was disturbing, and not just because his ear stuck to me. (Although, by no means do I want to diminish how disturbing that particular detail was.) Looking back, it seemed as though he'd been waiting for us, like he knew we were coming. There was also the ominous threat that we were being watched. But worst of all was the idea that there was a Level 2 zombie on the police force.

An L2 has no conscience, no sense of right and wrong. Combine that with the power of an NYPD badge and it's a terrifying mix.

Alex was oblivious to all of this when he finally arrived a couple minutes later. He gave us a funny look and asked, "What's wrong with you two? You don't look so good."

I still felt sick to my stomach, so I signaled Grayson to answer instead. He filled Alex in on what happened and by the time he was wrapping up the ear throwing portion of the story, I'd finally calmed down enough to talk.

"Are you sure he was a cop?" Alex asked. "And not just a security guard in a similar uniform?"

"Positive," I said. "He was NYPD."

"What does he look like?"

"Let's see, he's tall and spooky and . . . oh, yeah . . . he only has one ear," I snapped, even though Alex didn't deserve it. "Imagine Van Gogh but in a police uniform."

Alex ignored my attitude and kept asking questions. It's the type of focus that makes him a great Omega. He wanted to run through everything while it was still fresh in our minds. "Did he have a precinct number on his collar? A name tag under his badge?"

"I didn't notice any number," Grayson said. "But he did have a name tag. His name is Pell."

"That's good," Alex replied. "That's real good."

That's when I remembered another detail. "He also had a patch on his left shoulder. I noticed it when he turned to rip his ear off his head."

"What did the patch look like?"

I closed my eyes and tried to picture it fully in my mind. "It was red and had a dog on it, maybe more than one dog. I'm not sure. I got kind of distracted when he started peeling off his ear."

"A lot of the squads have their own patches," Alex said. "He could be with one of the K-9 units. I'll check with my uncle Paul to see if he can help."

Uncle Paul was a longtime police officer and a real father figure for Alex, whose actual father had almost no involvement in his life.

"Now for the most important question," Alex continued. "Are you two going to be okay?"

To be honest I wasn't sure. I took a deep breath, and despite my typical dislike of snow, the flakes falling on my face were cool and soothing. I just stood like that for a moment and then I said, "Yes, I'm okay."

"Me too," added Grayson.

"Good, because we're about to visit someone who's recovering from a serious zombie attack, and I don't want to get her worked up about another one. You saw her in the hospital. She's nowhere near full strength."

"You're right," I said.

"Should we even tell her about it?" asked Grayson.

Alex thought about this for a moment. "We'll see. For now let's just play it by ear."

It took me a second to get the joke.

"Oh . . . *by ear* . . . that's so funny," I said sarcastically.

Alex tried to keep from laughing as he said, "Just checking to make sure you still have your sense of humor."

Although Natalie lived on the twelfth floor, her family had temporarily moved downstairs so their apartment could be remodeled. Considering it was already the nicest apartment I'd ever seen, I couldn't imagine how they were improving it. But as someone who hates heights I was more than happy with the change. We took the stairs to the second floor and knocked on the door to 2-B.

"Check it out," Grayson said, pointing to the number. "Hamlet."

Alex gave him a curious look. "What do you mean Hamlet?"

"2-B," he said, as if this were obvious. "'*To be* or not *to be*, that is the question.' It's, like, the most famous line in the play."

"Have I ever told you that you're weird?" Alex asked.

"Yes," replied Grayson. "Frequently."

Natalie opened the door, but only part way, and peered out at us. Her face was pale and she had a confused, almost sleepy look in her eyes.

"Hey, Natalie, it's so great to see you up and out of the hospital bed," said Alex.

She cocked her head to the side and squinted as she studied him more closely. "Do I know you?"

It was devastating.

"Of course you do," he said. "I'm Alex. We've been friends for years. This is Grayson and Molly."

She studied our faces but didn't seem to recognize any of us. I was heartbroken. I think we'd assumed that since she'd been released from the hospital, she was doing better. Now we just stood there silently as we tried to think of what to say.

That's when she laughed.

"You guys are such suckers. You should see your expressions," she said as she finally opened the door all the way. "Welcome to the Hamlet Suite."

"That's not funny," Alex bellowed. "That's not funny at all."

"Ooooh," I mocked. "All of a sudden it's Mr. Comedian who doesn't have a sense of humor."

"By the way, did you hear what she called the apartment?" Grayson asked as he gave Alex a little poke in the shoulder. "The *Hamlet* Suite."

"That only proves that you're both weird," he replied.

I think it was the first time I'd laughed in weeks.

Once she stopped pretending she had amnesia, Natalie seemed more like her normal self, although her voice was still weak. We had gourmet hot chocolate that her mom special ordered from a café on the Upper West Side (It was ridiculously fancy, with shaved peppermint bark and marshmallow chunks, but it was beyond delicious) and we sat down in a family room that looked oddly familiar.

"Why do I feel like I've been here before?" Grayson asked, looking around.

"Because you kind of have," she said. "This apartment is ten floors directly below my apartment, so the layout is identical. My parents had everything brought down and put in the exact same place. Every room, every wall, every everything looks the same. Well, everything except for my room."

"Why's that?" I asked.

"It looks a little less bedroom and a little more intensive care unit," she said. "I guess it's an advantage of having surgeons as parents. They have access to lots of medical equipment."

She tried to play it off as a joke, but I could tell that it bothered her. In a weird way, though, it made me happy. Natalie's parents rarely made time for her in their busy lives. Maybe now, when she needed them most, they were finally coming through.

"Speaking of your parents," Alex said, "are they around?"

"Nope. Dad had to go to the hospital to check on a patient, and Mom is running some errands," she replied. "We've got about thirty minutes until she gets back, so let's start talking."

That gave us just enough time to talk all things Omega. It also let me tell them what I'd wanted to say since the stroke of midnight on New Year's Eve.

"Before we talk about anything else, there's something I need to say."

I took a deep breath and just tried to blurt it all out at once.

"I'm so sorry. I'm so breathtakingly sorry. Everything's my fault. I didn't just think Marek was dead, I was certain of it. I saw him fall from the top of the George Washington Bridge. There was no doubt in my mind. You all believed me . . . and I was wrong."

"Yeah," said Natalie. "About that. How did he survive the fall?"

16

"They rebuilt him," replied Alex. "They used body parts from his brother and cousins to make him whole again."

"Okay," Natalie said. "There goes my appetite for the rest of the day."

Then she looked right at me.

"So how is that *your fault*?"

It turned out she didn't blame me. None of them did. I don't know why. I mean, I still blamed myself, but it was an incredible relief.

Once I'd gotten my apology out of the way, we tried to fill in the blanks for Natalie about what happened that night. Not surprisingly, her memory was incomplete.

"How much do you remember?" asked Alex.

"Let's see," she said, straightening her posture. "I remember Molly calling us all to the steps in front of the library. And I remember the showdown in the old printing press room. There were a lot of bad guys and not so many good guys until Molly's mom and her Omega team arrived. Then there was a big fight, and that's where it starts to get fuzzy."

Grayson asked, "Do you remember who you were fighting?"

Natalie nodded. "I think it was the big redhead, right? Edmund."

"That's right," I said. "It was Edmund."

"So what happened to him after he was done with me?" she asked.

We exchanged glances for a moment before Grayson answered.

"Alex happened to him," he said.

"It was unbelievable," I added. "Edmund didn't even get to throw a punch. Alex saw what he did to you, and he unleashed the wrath of krav maga and killed him on the spot. And when the others saw what he did, they all pretty much ran away."

The memory of this quieted us all for a moment, until Natalie looked over at Alex and said, "Always my hero."

"That's funny, because a few minutes ago you didn't even recognize my face," he joked. They shared a look and it was pretty great. It was a look of total trust and friendship. During their time in Omega they had each saved the other too many times to count.

"So what's the plan?" she asked, breaking the moment.

"What do you mean?" I replied.

"Marek's back and Dead City is more dangerous than ever," she said. "How is Omega responding?"

The boys and I shared a nervous look, and then I turned back to Natalie.

"We're not," I said. "Omega has terminated all activity."

Through the Looking Glass

At first Natalie couldn't believe what she was hearing. She scanned our faces, looking for any glimmer of a smile or some other hint that we might be joking.

We weren't.

"Omega has terminated all activity?" She said it like it was some foreign phrase. "What does that even mean?"

"Exactly what it sounds like," Alex replied. "Everything and everybody is shut down."

"For how long?"

He shrugged. "Indefinitely."

We told her about an emergency team meeting we had with Dr. Hidalgo, during which he informed us that Omega had been too exposed. All Omegas past and present were in danger, and as a result the Prime O and the executive council had no other option but to enact what he called a "lockdown."

"He said there's even a chance it might never come back," added Alex.

"You had a team meeting?" she asked. "Without me? The team captain?"

"You weren't exactly in condition to meet," Alex reminded her. "Besides, you were sort of there."

"Yeah," I said with a half laugh, remembering how it all transpired. "We had to have it in the hallway right outside your room."

"And why is that?" she asked, still perturbed.

I looked at Grayson to see if he wanted to tell her, but he avoided eye contact, so I explained it instead. "Because Grayson refused to leave the hospital until you regained consciousness."

"Dr. H was not happy about it," Alex added in a total understatement. "He wanted a more private setting, but Grayson would not budge. G said he'd quit Omega before he'd leave. He stayed in that lobby for thirty-seven hours."

Natalie went to say something, but she stopped herself. This bit of information caught her completely off guard, and all the anger building up inside her drained in an instant. When she still couldn't think of the right words, she stood up silently, walked across the room to Grayson, and buried him in a hug.

I didn't always know where I fit in; but, with regard to the rest of my Omega team, Natalie was the brain, Alex was the muscle, and Grayson was always the heart.

That was the end of our Omega conversation. For the rest of our visit we just hung out and talked about less stressful things, like the foods Natalie planned to devour once her doctors cleared her to eat whatever she wanted. Spicy noodles and pepperoni pizza were high on the list. We made a list of where we wanted to go together. It was nice.

By the time we left, Nat looked worn-out and I worried that we'd stayed too long. On my way to the door, though, she pulled me aside for a private conversation.

"Any word from your mother?"

"Not since that night," I replied.

"Have you looked at the clock by the zoo?" she asked.

My mother and I had a secret spot near the Central Park Zoo where we left emergency messages for each other. Natalie had discovered it just before Christmas.

"I check every day," I answered. "But there hasn't been anything there."

Natalie thought this over and said, "Keep looking. I'm sure she'll reach out to you soon."

I nodded as though I agreed, but in truth I was more hopeful than confident.

"And when you do see her," Natalie continued, "tell her I said thanks. I don't remember much about New Year's Eve. But I remember her taking care of me. I'm pretty sure she saved my life."

"I'll tell her," I said. "Now you better get some rest."

I gave her an awkward hug, awkward because I still felt guilty about everything. The fact that my mother saved her life was a reminder that I had a hand in endangering it in the first place.

Alex, Grayson, and I walked to the subway station together. Or rather, Grayson and I walked together while Alex followed a few feet behind us, keeping an eye out for any evil one-eared police officers.

"Be safe," Alex instructed us when we split up to head to different platforms—he was going uptown toward the Bronx, while Grayson and I were riding toward Midtown.

"We will," I said. "I promise."

Grayson had been particularly quiet during our visit, and as we rode the C train I tried to figure out what was bothering him.

"So are you going to tell me what's the matter? Or am I going to have to guess?" I asked. "I think Natalie looked good."

He nodded. "Yeah. She did. Better than I expected."

"Then why do you seem so disappointed? That should make you happy."

"It does make me happy, but . . ." He hesitated for a moment before saying, "With that cop today. Did you see what I did when he ripped off his ear and threatened us?"

"No," I said. "What did you do?"

"Exactly," he replied. "I didn't do anything. I just stood there. Frozen."

"What are you talking about?" I said. "Neither of us did anything."

"Alex would have," he said. "It's just like Natalie said, he's always the hero. I don't know. I guess it's not in my DNA. I just don't have the . . . heroic gene or whatever it is."

"Did you miss the part where she hugged you and cried because she thought *you* were a hero?"

Grayson sighed and shook his head. "I'm loyal . . . but

Alex is brave. There's a huge difference. One you admire and one you depend on."

"No," I said. "You're not just loyal, you're also crazy. Because only a crazy person could draw that conclusion."

He shrugged.

We were almost to Thirty-Fourth Street, where I had to switch trains, so I didn't have much time to straighten out his thinking. That's when I remembered something Natalie told me right after I'd been attacked in the Roosevelt Island subway station.

"The very first day you and I met, when that L2 attacked me, do you know what Natalie said about you?"

"That I was good with computers?" he said lamely.

"No. She warned me not to underestimate you. She said that you were amazing, and she was right. So don't underestimate yourself. You're a total rock star, Grayson. Natalie knows it. Alex knows it. And I certainly know it. You should know it too."

He gave me a begrudging smile, although I couldn't tell if I had really solved the problem or just softened it for a moment.

The subway doors opened and I gave him one last look before I got off the train.

"Say it with me," I told him. "Rock star."

He laughed. "Go catch your train."

"Rock star," I said again as I exited onto the platform.

I lingered there to watch him pull away. I felt bad he thought that way, but I guess it wasn't that different than me blaming myself.

Ten minutes later I caught the train going to Queens. Except, I didn't ride it all the way home. Instead, I got off at Fifth Avenue so I could check for a message from my mother.

I had downplayed it when I was talking to Natalie, because I figured she had enough to worry about, but I was really nervous about my mom. The moment Marek returned, Mom was in danger. She should have run away right then, but she stayed with Natalie until the ambulance arrived. That gave the undead plenty of time to set a trap for her somewhere underground. Every day that had gone by without a message made me worry a little more that she hadn't been able to escape them.

Luckily, it had stopped snowing and the afternoon sun was peeking out from an otherwise gloomy sky. That meant there were people walking around the park, and I didn't stand out as much.

The Delacorte Clock is just past the entrance to the

zoo. It sits on a row of archways, and features sculptures of animals playing musical instruments. (My favorite is the penguin drummer.) Every hour and half hour the animals dance around as a nursery rhyme chimes.

It was twelve thirty and the clock was playing "Row, Row, Row Your Boat" when I slipped in alongside a group of tourists who had stopped to admire it.

I breathed a huge sigh of relief the moment I saw the message. It was a series of numbers written on a piece of masking tape stuck to the middle arch. If you weren't looking for it, you'd never notice it. And, even if you did see it, it wouldn't make sense unless you knew the basic Omega Code, which uses numbers that correspond with the periodic table of elements. They were:

13/53/58 49 74/8/60/68/57/60 8/10/61

Since (unlike my friends and me) you probably haven't memorized the periodic table inside out, I'll translate. The numbers correspond to the following elements: aluminum, iodine, cerium, indium, tungsten, oxygen, neodymium, erbium, lanthanum, neodymium again, oxygen again, neon, and promethium. If you write out all of their elemental symbols you get:

Al/I/Ce In W/O/Nd/Er/La/Nd O/Ne Pm

Alice's Adventures in Wonderland was one of my mother's favorite books. She used to read it to me at bedtime when I was little, and sometimes we'd visit the sculpture of Alice right there in Central Park. I was certain that's where Mom would be waiting for me at one p.m.

That was thirty minutes away, which gave me just enough time to take a couple of false turns and backtracks to make sure no one was following me. Considering my run-in with Officer Pell, I wanted to be extra careful.

It's funny how something you haven't thought about in ages will unexpectedly come back to you as clearly as if it happened yesterday. That's what happened as I was cutting back along a pathway and suddenly remembered my mother's favorite line from the book.

"It's no use going back to yesterday, because I was a different person then."

She loved that line and liked to quote it to me. She thought it was so smart, but at the time I didn't really understand why. Now, though, it made total sense. As much as I sometimes wish that I could go back and erase the mistakes I've made, I really am a different person now than I was just a few weeks ago. And I'm a very different person than I was before I became an Omega.

The sculpture of Alice is bronze and about twice the size of an actual person. It features her sitting on a giant mushroom, surrounded by the White Rabbit, the Cheshire cat, the Dormouse, and the Mad Hatter. One thing I've always loved about it is that you're allowed to climb up onto the mushroom and sit next to her.

I walked up to the sculpture, leaned against it, and waited. About five minutes later I saw my mother walking toward me. She wore black jeans, a black leather jacket, and a Yankees cap. She crossed the ground quickly, taking long, fast strides.

"Are you okay?" she asked with urgency as she neared me.

I nodded and she gave me a huge hug.

"I'm so sorry about what happened on New Year's," I said near tears.

"It wasn't your fault, baby. I thought he was dead too."

I started to cry. Not big tears, but tears. I was over-whelmed by everything that had happened. Right then, she wasn't a zombie killer, she was just my mom.

"What about you?" I said, clearing my throat. "Are you okay?"

"Yeah," she said. "There were a couple close calls, but I'm fine."

For a moment I just sat there and looked at her. Finally I asked, "Why did you put up the message?"

She gave me a perplexed look and asked, "What message?"

"On the Delacorte Clock. The message to meet here, right now."

Her expression changed as she considered this.

"I thought *you* put that message up," she replied, a sense of uneasiness taking over us both. We were being set up by someone who knew our code. Our eyes widened and we started to run away, but it was too late.

Marek Blackwell was walking right toward us.

Row, Row, Row Your Boat

My mom's first instinct was to shield me from Marek. She stepped forward to move directly between us, and subtly adjusted her stance so that her knees were bent and she was up on the balls of her feet, ready to fight.

"Now, now, there's no need for that," he said, holding up his hands in mini surrender. "This is a peaceful meeting."

One thing about Marek that always surprises me is his wardrobe. He doesn't dress like you'd expect an evil dark lord of the underground to dress. He wears sharp clothes like a successful businessman. This was a snowy Saturday afternoon, and while most of the people in the park were bundled up in jeans, sweaters, jackets, and knit caps, Marek wore a dress shirt, a black tie, and a dark burgundy overcoat with a fur collar. He even had on a fedora. If you randomly saw him in a crowd, he'd be the first person you'd trust. Let that be another reminder that you really can't judge a book by its cover.

"I have no desire to hurt either one of you," he continued.

He moved pretty well for a guy who'd been rebuilt with body parts from dead relatives, although he still had the limp I'd noticed on New Year's Eve.

"What if we want to hurt you?" asked my mother.

He stopped walking and looked right at her. "Well, then that's when these gentlemen would get involved."

He motioned to a group of four policemen who had taken strategic positions nearby. Each one wore the same red shoulder patch that Officer Pell had worn earlier in the day. This new partnership between Marek and the New York Police Department was troubling.

"I may not be at full strength," he said as he exaggerated his limp for a couple steps, "but these young men are a different story."

He stopped a few feet from us, maintaining a safe distance.

"Then what do you want?" asked my mom.

"What? No pleasantries? No hello? No 'So glad to see you didn't die when I threw you off the George Washington Bridge'?"

"You mean when you were trying to kill my daughter?"

He flashed a politician's smile. "You make a good point. I probably deserved that."

"I'll ask again," she said, agitation in her voice. "What do you want?"

"Peace," he answered. "I want peace. For more than a century the Omegas have hunted my friends and me, and I want that to end. Actually, let me rephrase that. I *insist* that it end. Don't let my current physical condition mislead you. If there's one thing New Year's should have demonstrated, it's that we are stronger than ever. I am building a better life for my people, and that can't happen as long as you continue to attack and harass us."

"You're forgetting something," said Mom. "You and I have been doing this for a long time. We have a history together and I know you can't be trusted."

"We have been doing it for a while," he said. "And I think we've both suffered greatly as a result. That's why I wanted to make this offer directly to you. If you and I can come to peace with each other, everyone else should be able to do the same. I think it's time we lead by example."

"So what's your offer?"

"We go our separate ways. It's as simple as that. My people will hurt none of yours and your people will leave us alone. All I'm asking is that you make your *lockdown* permanent."

I didn't like the fact that he used the same term, "lockdown," that we used in our private meetings. Somehow he was getting information from inside Omega.

"And what do we get in return?" Mom asked.

"You get to live normal lives," he said. "You get to be with your husband and your daughters. You no longer have to hide out in abandoned sewers and send secret messages with codes on clocks. My brother Milton can even go back to teaching children about science instead of training them to kill the undead."

"The brother you vowed to kill no matter what?" said Mom.

Marek thought about this for a moment. "That was more than a century ago," he said. "I'd like to think that our family could get past our differences and reunite."

Mom did not look like she believed any of this. "And if we don't accept your offer?"

"That would be a shame," he said. "Because from this point on any Omega activity will be considered an act of aggression, and we will respond with all-out war. War like you've never seen. Trust me when I say you don't want to face an undead army. Think about this: We knew you were coming to Times Square. We know about the lockdown. We even know the code you use to talk with your daughter."

He motioned toward the Alice sculpture and smiled.

"If you try to plan anything to get in our way, I'll know about that, too," he added. "And then it will be just like the Queen of Hearts . . . Off with your heads."

Rather than wait for a response, he turned and walked away. I noticed his limp didn't seem as bad as before, and I wondered how much of it had been an act. The policemen joined him and escorted him down the path away from us.

My mother watched silently until they were out of sight, and then she turned to me. I could tell she was thinking through everything.

"What are we going to do?" I asked.

"Exactly what he told us to do," she said. "They know too much about us and we have no idea what they're up to. We have no choice but to remain on lockdown."

"Undead army," I said, repeating the two words that had most caught my attention.

"How terrifying is that?" she said.

I looked up at my mom and studied her face for a moment. "Do you think he meant it?"

"Meant what?"

"That we could go back to normal? That our family could be together? Because . . . that would be incredible."

She closed her eyes for a moment before answering. "That *would* be incredible. But he'll never let it happen. He's planning something. Something huge. I don't know what it is. But I know he's not planning on us being happy. And I guarantee you that he won't be satisfied until I'm dead."

"If he wants you dead, then why didn't he just attack you here and now? They had us outnumbered."

"That's a good question," she said. "I think it's because there's someone he hates even more than me."

It took me a second to figure out whom she was talking about. "His brother! He hates Milton. So you don't think he meant it when he said they could go back to being brothers?"

"No, I don't. I think this meeting had two purposes. He wanted to deliver his threat, but more importantly he wanted to have someone follow me to see if I'll lead him to Milton's hiding place."

"You think there's someone here in the park watching us?" I asked.

"I don't think it," she said. "I know it."

"Wait," I said. "Don't tell me yet. Let me see if I can figure it out."

I tried to be inconspicuous as I scanned the people in the park, looking for anyone who might be spying on us. It took me about a minute.

"I see him," I said. "Red jacket on the bench, reading a book."

"Very good," she replied. "How do you know?"

"I recognize him from earlier," I explained. "He was sitting on a bench by the clock when I found the message."

"I don't think he's alone, though," she said. "Check out the woman pushing the baby stroller. She's already walked by twice. She never checks on her baby, but she makes eye contact with the man on the bench every minute or two."

"So what's our plan?"

"They want to find a secret underground passageway," she said. "Let's make them think that's where we're going."

My mother started walking and I followed right behind her. We walked right past the man on the bench, and I'll tell you this, he was cool. He didn't look up or move. He just read his book like he was totally engrossed.

I was careful not to make eye contact, so I looked down

at his feet as we passed him. He was wearing dark blue running shoes with mud stains at the toes.

"You can't tell anyone what I'm about to show you," Mom said to me in a whisper that was just loud enough for him to overhear. "It's a new entrance to the underground." That's when I noticed the man flinch ever so slightly. She'd baited the hook perfectly.

"How do you get there?" I asked.

She waited until we were out of his earshot, and she answered quietly, "I'm still working on that. We need someplace secluded where we can turn the tables on them."

Here's a fun fact. It turns out that I have a habit of humming whenever I get nervous. (Of course, I never noticed this until one day when Alex pointed it out, and now I can never *not* notice it!) So I started humming the last song I'd heard: "Row, Row, Row Your Boat."

Mom stopped for a second and looked right at me. "Molly, that's a great idea."

I was glad I helped; I just wished I knew what I'd done. "*What's* a great idea?"

"Row Your Boat," she said. "We'll lead them to the boathouse."

There's a lake in the middle of Central Park called The Lake. (Really clever name, huh?) And a popular activity is for people to go out on it in rowboats they rent at Loeb Boathouse, which sits at the end of a long dock next to a restaurant. But it was winter and the lake was frozen.

"I don't think the boathouse is open," I said.

Mom picked up the pace ever so slightly. "That's what makes it perfect."

The boathouse is a square wooden building that looks like a garage with a weather vane on the top. It extends out over the water so that you can literally row in and park your boat. Now that the lake was frozen, there was a gap about three feet high that separated the bottom of the boathouse from the ice.

This gap was how Mom planned to get inside.

"Wait until I'm all the way in before you follow me," she said. "We're still pretty early in the winter, and I want to make sure the ice is strong enough to hold us."

The mere thought of crashing through the ice was enough to slow me down. Mom walked to the edge and put one foot out onto the slippery surface, whispering a near silent prayer, "Please don't break."

It didn't.

Once she knew it was strong enough, she quickly slid under the bottom and climbed up into the building. She made it look easy and I followed her.

"Good job," she said when I popped up inside next to her.

I sat there for a moment, my feet dangling over the edge of the slip where the boats pulled in. The inside of the building looked a lot like my grandparents' attic. There was stuff crammed everywhere, long wooden oars, dingy orange life jackets, and a pair of overturned rowboats.

"Get under there and hide," she said, pointing at one of the boats.

"Why am I hiding?"

"Because I want them to think that we've gone underground. They'll look through that window before they come in, and if they see us in here, they'll know we're on to them."

She lifted up the edge of the boat and I reluctantly crawled under it. When she set it back down, I was plunged into darkness. The combination of dark and damp, frozen and slippery made it the least comfortable place I'd ever been.

"Don't come out unless I call your name," she said.

"Seriously?"

"I mean it," she said. "We play by my rules."

"All right," I whined.

Because the edge of the boat was curved, I could peek out from the bottom. (Although I had to press my cheek against the frozen floorboards to do it.) It took about thirty seconds or so for my eyes to adjust to the darkness, but I was able to see a reflection of the room in a row of silver paint cans along the wall. The round shape of the cans distorted everything like one of those mirrors you see at a carnival, but at least I had some idea what was going on. I could see my mom squeeze into a narrow area between a cabinet and the rear wall. The distortion made her look super skinny and about eight feet tall.

For the next few minutes everything in the boathouse was silent and still, except for the sound of wind racing across the ice and whistling through the slats in the floor. I was cold and shivering like I was in some bad ghost story. First we heard the approaching footsteps, and next there was talking outside. Then someone started to push the door.

They were coming in.

Ice Breakers

I kept perfectly still in my hiding place beneath the rowboat, my pulse quickening as they tried to force their way in. Rather than coming in from underneath the boathouse like we did, they were trying to break through the main door. After about fifteen seconds of grunting and straining, there was a loud pop and the door burst open. A shaft of sunlight cut across the room for as long as it took the two of them to enter and close the door behind them. Once they did, everything returned to darkness and my eyes had to readjust.

"Check for any access that leads underground," the man told his partner. "I overheard her say it was a new entrance."

I squinted to make out their reflections in the paint cans as they rifled through all the clutter. He was poking around a pile of life jackets and she was pulling back a large canvas cover, when someone new joined the conversation.

"You're not going to find what you're looking for."

The voice belonged to my mother, and it had the same startling effect on them that it had had on me when I was eight years old and trying to see if there were any Christmas presents hidden under her bed.

"If either of you wants to make it out of here," she said, "I recommend you start talking and tell me what Marek's planning."

I had a good view of Mom as she stepped in front of the doorway and blocked their escape. She had a long metal tool with a hook at the end that she held like a weapon.

"Do you honestly think you can handle the two of us by yourself?" asked the man, who had apparently forgotten that my mom was not alone when she entered the boathouse. I'll be honest. I was offended.

"Oh, I can handle you two," Mom said confidently. "I'm just trying to figure out if a worse punishment might be to let you both live. That way you can go back and tell Marek that you ruined his one chance of finding Milton. How do you think he'll react to that?"

That got him angry and he charged her, slamming her against the wall. She pushed back with the metal tool and spun it around so that the hook cut right into his gut. She jerked it up and down before she pulled it out of him.

You'd think that would've finished him off, but it didn't. He flashed a wicked grin and was completely unfazed by the purple goo oozing from his stomach. Just seeing it in the reflection was gross enough. I'm pretty sure if I saw it up close it would've made me want to hurl.

They traded a couple punches before the woman called out. "Wait a second. What about the girl she was with?"

Finally, somebody noticed I wasn't there.

I could tell by her voice that she was right next to the boat I was hiding under. Since my element of surprise was about to disappear, I decided to be bold.

I rolled over onto my back and tucked my knees all the way up to my chest. Then I pushed up with my legs as hard as I could against the boat so that it flipped over and hit her. She staggered back and tried to get her balance, but there was a problem. She was on the edge of the slip, so when she stepped back there was no floor. She fell and slammed right onto the frozen lake.

"I'm pretty sure I told you to wait until I called your name," Mom said angrily. "You never listen."

Would it have killed her to say, "What a cool move that was, Molly?"

I was about to say something snarky right back at her, when I saw the look of horror on her face. I ducked just as a long wooden oar swung right by my head and missed me by no more than an inch or two. The man laughed as he took another swing at me, but this time I was able to deflect it with an oar that I had just picked up.

It looked like we were about to have a swordfight with the oars, but then I felt a tug at my ankle. It was the woman reaching up and grabbing me. She jerked hard and I came crashing down on her and the ice.

That's when I heard the terrifying sound of ice cracking. I couldn't see where it was and I had no idea how long it would be before it broke. I wasn't planning on waiting around to learn the answer.

I scrambled up onto my feet, and after slipping a couple times, managed to reach up to the edge of the deck. I started to pull myself up, but she grabbed me and pulled me back onto the ice.

She squeezed me tight and whispered in my ear, "I hope you're a good swimmer." For the record, you'd think it'd be scarier when zombies yelled and moaned at you, but my personal experience is that it's far worse when they whisper.

I tried to break free, but she spun me around and landed an elbow into my jaw that sent me sprawling across the ice.

I looked up and saw my mom. She wanted to help, but she had a problem of her own. Despite all the purple ooze coming out of his stomach, the man was still putting up a good fight.

"It's been fun and all," said Mom, "but we're going to wrap this up."

She picked up one of the cans of paint and slammed it up into his chin. He tried to say something, but instead of words there were just some brief gurgling noises before black liquid started pouring from his mouth. A second later his body dropped right in front of her. He was dead.

Meanwhile, I'd managed to get back to my feet, but the woman was still blocking my way back up off the ice, which was cracking even more.

"A little help!" I called out.

"Pulley!" shouted my mom.

I looked up and saw that there was a pulley directly above me. Normally it was used to help lift boats out of the water, but now it was my escape route.

I jumped straight up and grabbed onto it. Then, as the woman charged at me to pull me back down I did a double scissor kick and hit her in the head with each foot. She collapsed to the ice, dazed but not dead. That is, not until my mother pushed a rather large anchor over the edge of the slip and directly onto her. First the anchor smashed through the zombie, and then it broke through the ice as both of them sank down into the freezing water.

I hung there for a moment, my sneakers dangling less than a foot above the icy lake as I tried to catch my breath.

"Can you make it?" asked my mom as she reached out for me.

I swung my body back and forth a couple times until I got close enough for her grab my legs and pull me to safety.

We both plopped down onto the floor.

"You okay?" she asked.

I smiled. "I'm better than okay. How about you?"

"Well, you know how much I love it when we get to share these mother-daughter moments."

We both laughed.

"It may not be a normal family," I said, "but it's our family. This is what we do. This is who we are."

"You got that right," said Mom.

She turned her attention to the man and rolled him over onto his back. The massive stomach wound was actually more disgusting than I imagined, but I was too tired to get sick.

"Let's see what clues you have for us," she said as she

started checking the pockets of his coat and pants. She pulled out a phone, a wallet, and the paperback that he'd been reading.

She handed me the book and started digging through his wallet.

"Defending Manhattan," I said, looking at the cover. "New York City during the Revolutionary War. Sounds boring."

"We have a name," Mom said as she pulled out his ID. "Herman Prothro. West Eighty-Eighth Street."

She looked up at me. "That's a nice neighborhood."

"So he's a rich zombie," I said. "Any idea what Herman Prothro does? I mean, other than read boring books and attack Omegas."

She pulled out a business card and held it up to the light to read it better. "It says that he's the vice president of the Empire State Tungsten Company."

We shared a confused look for a moment before I asked, "What's the Empire State Tungsten Company?"

"I don't know," she answered as she flashed a grin. "But I think they need a new vice president."

She rolled him off of the wooden floor and he splashed through the hole in the ice. There was another gurgling, not unlike the one he made when he died, and then some bubbles as his body disappeared into the darkness.

We exited through the door they had busted open and walked in the park together for about forty-five minutes, until Mom felt confident that there were no other zombies following us.

Our walk ended up behind the Metropolitan Museum of Art looking out over the Great Lawn. Because of the cold weather there was hardly anyone on it, but during spring and summer the Great Lawn becomes the ultimate New York picnic destination.

"Do you remember when we used to come out here?" she asked. "Those amazing lunches that your dad made?"

"Of course I do," I said. "Those are some of my favorite memories ever."

"Mine too," said Mom. "I want those to be the memories you have of me. Not images of me killing zombies in some freezing boathouse. I want you to remember me as a mother sitting on that blanket, reading stories to you."

"Like Alice in Wonderland?" I said.

"Exactly. Remember me as the mom who read Alice in Wonderland to you."

"It's no use going back to yesterday, because I was a different person then," I said, quoting her favorite line.

She smiled. "You still remember that too?"

"I'll always remember that. And now I finally understand it. I can't go back to being that girl on the blanket. I was a different person then."

"I guess you were," she replied. "I guess we all were different people."

She hugged me tight and I lingered in her arms.

"I don't know how long it's going to be until we see each other again," she said, sadness in her voice. "I'm going to have to hide deep."

"I know," I said. "What should we do about Omega?"

"Nothing. Nothing unless you hear different directly from me. Until then Omega is done."

I nodded.

"I mean it, Molly. It can't be like the boathouse, where you're supposed to wait for me but you don't."

"Okay," I said. "But that was a pretty cool move, wasn't it?"

She laughed.

"It was the coolest move I ever saw. But I still mean it."

"I know."

"I love you, Molly Koala," she said, calling me by the nickname I hadn't heard in ages.

"I love you, Mom."

La Traviata

O pera? Are you serious?"

We were less than fifteen seconds into family night, and my sister Beth was already protesting the music that filled the apartment.

"Show some respect for your heritage," Dad said as he handed her some bell peppers and a cutting board. "And chop these while you're at it."

"We're only a quarter Italian," she replied. "What about the parts of our heritage that made music, I don't know, in the last century?"

"You may only be a quarter Italian, but Molly's a quarter too and I'm half," he said. "Two quarters and a half, what does that add up to, Molls?"

"One whole Italian," I said, playing along with Dad's logic.

"There you go. There's an entire Italian person in this kitchen, so be polite," he said with a cheesy Italian accent. "Besides, you know the rules. Tonight's my night and I get to pick."

The rules of family night are simple but firm. Every month we each get one evening to plan. It can be anything, as long as we're all together. And to encourage fresh ideas, we're supposed to be open to new things . . . like opera.

When Dad's in charge of family night we often end up in the kitchen. I think he likes it for a couple reasons. First of all, he's a great cook and wants to make sure Beth and I learn the basics. But more importantly, he likes the way it squishes us all into a small space and forces us to talk and share as we literally bump into each other.

That night we were making kitchen sink spaghetti, which has nothing to do with the sink and gets its name from the fact that Dad puts "everything but the kitchen sink" into the sauce. He thought opera was the perfect addition. But rules or not, he didn't want Beth to be miserable, so he gave her a possible escape.

"How about this?" he said. "I'm going to tell you a story about this opera and once I'm done, if you still want me to turn it off, I will."

"Why don't you save yourself the trouble and turn it off now?" she said with a sly smile. "Because I guarantee my opinion's not going to change."

"Maybe, but that's not the deal," he said. "I get to tell my story first. Then you decide."

She was suspicious, but didn't really have much choice. "Okay, fine."

"You have to keep cooking, though," he said. "Both of you."

We had specific jobs to do so that everything would come together perfectly. Beth was chopping vegetables, and I was stirring and seasoning the tomato sauce while Dad sautéed some Italian sausage. The combination of the sizzle and the smell was incredible.

"We're cooking," Beth said. "Start talking."

"Okay, your mom and I had been dating for about two and a half months . . ."

I knew then and there that Dad was going to win this argument.

". . . and one day she told me she was planning to see *La Traviata* at the Met." He turned from the stove for a

52

second to explain to Natalie. "'The Met' is what we cultured people call the Metropolitan Opera House at Lincoln Center."

She didn't miss a beat and came right back at him. "'The Met' is also what you call the Metropolitan Museum of Art. You'd think for cultured people you'd be able to come up with different nicknames for different places."

"That's funny. I never noticed that." Dad said laughing. "Anyway, your mother was going to go with her sister, Fiona, no doubt because she assumed I was a caveman unable to enjoy something as sophisticated as opera. Now, I couldn't let her think that, so I told her that it was too bad she was going with someone else, because I loved opera."

"Was that true?" I asked.

"No. I didn't know anything about opera except what I'd learned from Bugs Bunny. But I didn't want her to know that. Then she threw me a curve. She said that Fiona didn't really want to go and asked if I wanted to go with her instead."

"Uh-oh."

"No kidding. Of course I said yes, but I was in full panic mode. I was worried I wouldn't understand anything because it's all sung in Italian. I was worried that I was going to prove that I was, in fact, an uncultured caveman.

So I spent three weeks studying everything there was to know about *La Traviata*. I memorized the characters, the plot, famous performances . . . I even knew the English translations of all the song titles. My plan was simple. I was going to dazzle her. But I had a problem."

"What?" I asked.

"I was so focused on studying that I didn't realize I was scheduled to work that night. I had to swap with someone at the last minute just so I could go on the date. I ended up working back-to-back shifts, and by the time we got to the Met I was already pretty tired."

Although her back was turned toward Dad as she chopped, I noticed that Beth was now closely following the story.

"Don't tell me you fell asleep," I said. "Did you snore?"

"I didn't snore . . . but I may have nodded off a little during the first act," he said with a smile. "I was just going to close my eyes for a second, but the next thing I know, there was applause. That woke me right up. It was intermission and I was worried that she was onto me so I just jumped right into my analysis. I talked about everything that I had studied. I could tell she was impressed.

I did a better job staying awake in the second act, and when it was over I picked up right where I left off. She couldn't believe how emotional I got as I talked about the tragic ending. I will never forget the look she gave me, hanging on every word I said. Even I almost believed that I was smart and cultured. We were right there next to the big fountain in Lincoln Center, surrounded by all those people in tuxedos and gowns and I had pulled it off . . . until I saw it."

"What?" asked Beth, now fully engrossed.

"A giant banner advertising that night's performance of . . . *Il Trovatore*."

We all started laughing, Dad loudest of all.

"You did not?" I squealed.

"Oh, I did. I totally learned the wrong opera. *Il Trovatore*, *La Traviata*, the names sound so much alike and they're both by Verdi. Everything I said had been wrong and your mother just went along with it. She knew what I'd done the second I started talking at intermission, and she just would not embarrass me. I should have known better than to think that I could put one over on her."

Now Beth turned from the counter to face him, a wide smile on her face. "So how did she respond once the truth was out there?"

"Not like I would have expected," he said. "She figured that if I tried that hard, it must mean that I really cared about her. And I realized that if she was going to go along with it just so she wouldn't embarrass me, well, that's when I knew I was in love. And seven months later when I proposed, I did it right at that fountain."

He let the story simmer for a moment as he brushed a little garlic onto the sausage. Then he gave her a sly look over his shoulder and said, "But we can always turn it off."

Beth just shook her head. "It's fine. We can keep listening."

I had never heard that story before and I loved it. It had been more than two months since that day with Mom in the boathouse. I thought about what she said afterward, about how she wanted me to remember her. She wanted me to think of her as a mother reading stories on a picnic blanket. And here was another memory, of a young woman falling in love. I'm sure this is how my dad pictures her.

Needless to say, the spaghetti was delicious and the dinner was great fun. Beth told us about a job she was applying for to work as a counselor at a drama camp run by the parks department.

"That sounds great," said Dad.

"If I get it," she said, "we'll put on three different plays during the summer."

"No operas?"

"No operas." She laughed.

"That reminds me," Dad said, turning to me. "Have you thought about what play you want to see for your birthday? I want to make sure we get good tickets."

For years we'd celebrated my birthday by going out to dinner and a Broadway show. It was great, and something I really loved. But the truth is, one of the reasons it became a tradition was because I never had enough friends to have a party. This year, though, things were different.

"Actually," I said, a little worried about how he might react. "I was thinking of having a party instead."

"I thought you loved Broadway."

"I do. It's just that I'd kind of like to do something with Alex, Grayson, and Natalie."

Right then the opera music hit a particularly dramatic moment, and Dad pretended to be the character as he lip-synched for a few seconds. "He's so sad because his daughters are leaving him for drama camp and parties with friends."

Beth and I both rolled our eyes.

"Just kidding," he said. "What kind of party do you want to have?"

This is where I was stumped. I knew I wanted to have one, I just didn't have any experience as to what one might be like.

"I don't know. Do you have any ideas?"

"We can get a clown or a magician. If you want I can get you all a tour of the fire house and you can slide down the pole."

"Yes, Dad," Beth said, exasperated. "She's turning six and she's wants a clown and a magician. Or better yet, we can get her a fairy princess."

"I'm sensing sarcasm," Dad joked. "Do you have any suggestions, Beth?"

"Yeah," I said eagerly. "You've got a lot more experience with . . . you know, being with people who are having a good time."

Beth absently twirled a forkful of spaghetti on her plate as she thought it over. "You want something fun but easy. Good for guys and girls. With low social pressure that will provide lasting memories."

"Yes, yes, and yes," I said. "I want a party that's all those things. And I especially like the fact that there isn't any clown or magician. Although, sliding down the pole in the fire house actually did sound kind of fun."

"As fun as Coney Island?"

Coney Island is awesome. It's a collection of amusement parks, roller coasters, and attractions all along the boardwalk in Brooklyn. It was the perfect party suggestion.

"That's it," I said. "That's exactly what I want to do."

"I like it too," Dad said. "It's been a couple years since I rode the Cyclone."

Beth and I both gave him a look, and he took the hint.

"Of course, you were probably thinking of just the kids riding the rides."

"I'll ride with you, Dad," said Beth. "And after that we can listen to some of *my* music."

"Gee," he said in his goofy dad voice, "I wonder which will make me dizzier."

It wasn't until later, after we'd finished putting away the dishes, that I saw the envelope. It had arrived in the mail that day and was addressed to me. I couldn't remember the last time I'd gotten an actual letter, so I was excited.

I opened it in my room, but rather than a letter there was a folded piece of paper and a small article clipped from a newspaper. The article was dated a week earlier and was about our favorite evil lord of the undead, Marek Blackwell.

It said Marek and the mayor had negotiated a deal for him to take control of some of the city's abandoned subway stations. His plan was to turn these ghost stations into underground entertainment complexes with restaurants, shops, and even some apartments. He called it RUNY, Reinventing Underground New York.

In the article it was hailed as a vision for the future, turning unused space into something good. But I knew something else. Underground and surrounded by Manhattan schist, these entertainment complexes would be the ultimate destination for zombies.

In a way it was kind of genius. Marek said he was trying to build a better life for the undead. This actually did that. As I considered this, I looked at the paper and saw a single question written with blue felt tip pen in block letters. It said:

WHERE IS HE GETTING THE MONEY TO DO THIS?

The Equinox

One of the great things about having a dad who's an amazing cook is that the leftovers that make their way into your lunch tend to be much better than those of your classmates. So, unlike the other kids who'd brown-bagged it and brought PB and Js or tuna fish sandwiches, I was savoring every bite of a rosemary chicken panini. Dad even packed a sweet and spicy dipping sauce with it. It was the kind of lunch that could inspire jealousy. At least, it could have if I hadn't been eating alone.

You see, of the roughly five hundred students at the Metropolitan Institute of Science and Technology, I was the only one who thought it was a good day to eat outside. MIST is a science magnet school that draws kids from all over New York City. They're really smart, certainly smart enough to know that you don't sit outside when it's almost freezing. And though the gothic buildings that make up the campus look like they belong in a horror movie, the view from the picnic tables is nice enough that I was willing to ignore the temperature.

I was nibbling on my sandwich and watching a red-and-white tugboat push a barge up the East River, when I heard footsteps approach from behind. I didn't even have to look to see who it was. Grayson's walk is distinctive: He goes fast until he's almost there, then nearly comes to a full stop and takes a breath before taking the final few steps at regular speed. It's like he's always in a hurry but never wants you to know it.

"Hey, G," I said as I took another bite and kept watching the tug do its job.

"Hey, Molly," he said warily. "How are you doing?"

"Fantastic," I replied, maybe a bit more enthusiastically than the situation warranted. "I've got a great lunch. I've got a great view. What more could I want?" I turned and looked right at him, trying my best to punctuate my enthusiasm with a convincing smile.

"You do realize that it's . . ."

"Check the calendar," I said, cutting him off. "Today is March twentieth, the first day of spring. Spring. As in no longer winter. As in it's totally appropriate to eat on the patio."

"Yeah, but if you check a thermometer," he replied, "it's like . . . forty-seven degrees."

I'll admit that I was being a bit irrational, but it had been more than two months since the boathouse. Sixty-four days, to be exact. And despite some occasional fun moments like family night, they had been sixty-four frustrating days.

There hadn't been any contact from my mother or the slightest hint that Omega might get called back into action. Even worse, there were signs that my friend group was having problems, and, as if all that wasn't enough, it had also been the coldest and snowiest winter in more than two decades.

There was nothing I could do about the first two, and my total lack of social skills left me clueless as to how to fix the third. So I figured the least I could do was celebrate the end of winter. Even if, meteorologically speaking, Mother Nature wasn't cooperating.

"I really am fine, Grayson," I said. "I just . . . can't spend another lunch period in that cafeteria. I guess I need fresh air more than I need heat."

He set his lunch on the table and sat down right next to me. "Works for me."

This is what makes Grayson such a great friend. He was willing to sit out in the cold not because it made sense, but because it made sense to me. And on this day that was just the kind of friend I needed most.

I took a bite of my panini and said, "Thank you."

He shrugged as if to say it was no big deal.

But it was a big deal. Everything about my friends was. I'd never had a group of friends before this school year, and part of me had always worried that I might never have one. But then Omega found me, and suddenly I had three amazing people whom I could literally trust with my life.

At first glance our foursome seemed like an unlikely grouping. There was glamorous and beautiful Natalie with her chic apartment on the Upper West Side, quiet and athletic Alex whose accent and swagger were straight out of the Bronx, Grayson the megabrain computer geek who lived with his professor parents in a Brooklyn brownstone, and good old awkward me, that weird Bigelow girl from Astoria, Queens.

I'm sure some people wondered why we hung out together. But that's because they couldn't possibly know the big thing we all had in common. It was our job to police and protect the zombies of New York. We were the ones who maintained the peace between the living and the undead. Omega made all of our differences insignificant.

And that was the problem.

Now that Omega was on lockdown, our group had begun to drift apart. We didn't have a case to work on or a problem to solve. We didn't have a reason to be together. And on top of that, Natalie's recovery was going slowly. At first she only came back to school for half days, which meant we rarely saw her. And when she finally did return full-time, she had so much make-up work to do she usually skipped lunch and went straight to the library.

I knew these were all good reasons, but part of me felt like she was avoiding us, or more specifically, avoiding me. Since I didn't have much experience in social situations, I tried to come up with ways to reassure myself that it was all in my imagination. My birthday party was going to be one of them.

"Hey, my birthday's in a couple weeks and I was thinking of having a little party out at Coney Island. Do you think you could come?"

Grayson was midchew so he had to swallow a bite of his no doubt inferior sandwich before answering, "Sure, that'd be great."

I looked back toward the river and asked, "You think she'll come?"

He could read my uncertainty and knew exactly what I was talking about.

"I think she's struggling," he said. "She's used to being the smartest and the strongest, and this is all new to her. But I do think she'll come. You're her good friend, Molly."

I just kept looking off into the distance and nodded. I thought about telling him about the newspaper article that had come in the mail, but before I could decide, someone else joined us.

"Hey, you guys realize that it's cold out here, right?" Alex said as he sat across the table from me.

"Really?" I joked. "I hadn't noticed."

"Vernal equinox," Grayson said, using the scientific term for the first day of spring. "We're celebrating."

Alex laughed.

"Speaking of celebrating, we were just talking about my birthday party. It's in a couple weeks. We're going to Coney Island. Interested?"

"In hot dogs and roller coasters? Always."

I felt a little stupid. I had worried that we were drifting apart, but neither one of them hesitated before saying they wanted to come to my party. I think I sometimes (okay, maybe always) make stuff like this harder than it should be.

"And guess what," he added. "I've got an early birthday

present." He unzipped his backpack and pulled out a small catalog. "My uncle Paul brought this over last night, and I thought you might want to look at it."

He handed it to me.

"It's the uniform catalog for the NYPD," he continued. "It's got everything from shirts and jackets to special belts that hold all their gear. In the back is a section with all the different squad patches. You can look to see if you recognize the one the psycho cop who ripped off his ear was wearing."

I hesitated. "We're not supposed to do anything Omega," I said, unsure if this counted.

"I don't think this is Omega," he said. "Some guy threatened you two and we want to know a little more about him. We're not on a case and we're not going to do anything about it. We're just trying to protect ourselves, which is the point of the lockdown in the first place."

I turned to Grayson, who added, "I think he's right."

"Okay," I said as I started flipping through the pages. The patches were located in the back, and there were more than I would have guessed. There was a fire truck for the emergency squad and an antique car for the auto crime division. My favorite was the patch for the mounted division, which had a horse on it.

I remembered that the patch I saw that day had a dog on it, but I wasn't sure if it was one dog or more than one. There was a picture of a German shepherd on the K-9 unit patch and a Labrador retriever on the bomb squad patch, but neither was like the one I had seen.

Then I turned the page and realized why I had been confused about the number. It's because the patch had one dog with three heads.

"That's it," I said, pointing and turning the catalog so that they both could see. "The red one with the three-headed dog."

Grayson recognized it instantly. "That's Cerberus."

I had no idea what he was talking about. "Who or what is Cerberus?"

"He's from Greek mythology," Grayson said. "Cerberus is the hellhound who guards the entrance to the underworld. He craves living flesh, so only the dead can get past him."

"Not exactly one of those feel-good myths, is it?" I said.

"Hardly any of them are," he replied.

Alex took the catalog and looked at it. "It says here that the patch is for the Departmental Emergency Action Deployment Squadron. Sounds like some sort of quick response unit for disasters and emergencies."

Grayson practically jumped out of his chair as he figured

something out. "That's what it sounds like," he said. "Unless you only look at the initials. D-E-A-D. It's the Dead Squad."

We were all quiet for a moment while we thought about this one.

"And their symbol is the evil creature that protects the underworld from the living," added Alex. "That's disturbing."

"That would explain so much," I said. "Remember when I told you about Marek surprising me and Mom?"

"You mean when you killed those two Level 2s in the boathouse?" asked Grayson. "It would be pretty hard to forget."

"Well, the cops that were with him had the same patch. What if there's a whole Dead Squad made up of zombie cops?"

I can't describe the feeling that I had at that moment. We were discussing zombies on the police force, which was terrible. But the conversation was thrilling. This is what we'd been missing. It was the first time I'd felt that kind of excitement since New Year's.

"How could Marek possibly pull that off?" asked Grayson. "This is not some secret underground group roaming around abandoned tunnels beneath the city. We're talking about a squadron within the New York City Police Department. It's a huge public organization."

It did seem far-fetched, and I wondered if maybe we

were jumping to conclusions because we wanted there to be some secret we could solve. We wanted it to be thrilling. But then Alex remembered something.

"Blue Moon," he said. "Operation Blue Moon had very specific goals. The undead wanted to infect the mayor, the archbishop and . . ."

". . . the chief of police," Grayson and I both said.

Alex nodded. "If they turned the chief of police into a zombie, he could easily set up a squadron and handpick who was placed on it."

The three of us were quiet as we considered the magnitude of what this might mean. My mom was right. Marek was up to something big, and we had no idea what it was.

Our little puzzle solving session was exhilarating, but it ended with a dull thud. There was nothing we could do about it. There was no one we could tell. I couldn't even try to get word to my mother, because Marek knew about our secret code on the Delacorte Clock. It did, however, give me something new to talk to Natalie about.

After school I looked for her among the crowd of students heading toward the Roosevelt Island Tram, which was her typical route home. But she wasn't with them. Instead I caught a glimpse of her a block away, heading toward the subway station.

I hurried to catch up, but just when I was close enough to call out her name, I saw the strangest thing. While she waited to cross the street, a man in a red hoodie walked right up behind her and slipped a folded piece of blue paper into a pocket on her backpack. Then he kept walking in a different direction.

It was lightning fast and I wouldn't have noticed it if I hadn't been focused right on her. Even still I might have doubted my own eyes if the man hadn't turned for a second, giving me a look at his face.

It was Liberty.

There was no way that was a coincidence.

Liberty was a friend, but he was more than that. He was an Omega and he was undead. More than anyone we knew, he lived in both worlds. On New Year's Eve he'd been part of my mother's team, the ones who rescued us. But he also was a part of the undead community, known for giving speeches about zombies' rights at flatline parties.

He was being secretive, which made me think he was reaching out to her on Omega business. That made sense, because she was our captain. I was excited, thinking it meant we were being called into action. But then I saw her meet up with a girl I'd never seen before. It was obvious that the girl had been waiting for her.

They entered the subway station together, and I followed from a safe distance. As she rode down the escalator, Natalie pulled out the piece of paper and read it. Then she showed it to the other girl.

If it was a communication about Omega, then she only would have shown it to another Omega.

That's when I figured out what was happening. There was only one explanation that made sense. Omega was no longer in a lockdown. I was just locked out. Natalie had already moved on to a new team. That would explain why she never had time to meet up after school. I wondered if Grayson and Alex were part of her new team as well, or if they'd been left behind like me.

I stayed on the upper level of the station and spied on them as they blended in with the crowd on the platform. When everybody else boarded the subway, they lingered behind.

I stepped behind a pillar so they couldn't see me. Once they thought the coast was clear, they hopped down by the tracks and started walking into the tunnel toward Manhattan.

I just stood there and watched, tears forming in my eyes as they disappeared into the darkness. Not only was I losing a friend, but I was also losing Omega.

The Hollow Men

The MIST library is a two-story stone building that sits on the quad between the Upper and Lower Schools. It looks like a little church, which is why most students call it "the chapel." I found Natalie sitting in the back at a big wooden table strewn with papers and books.

"That looks like a lot of work," I said.

"It is." Natalie seemed genuinely happy to see me. "Do you know anything about the poetry of T. S. Eliot?"

"No."

"That makes two of us," she replied as she started digging through the piles of paper. "Unfortunately, one of us has a critical analysis of it due on in Ms. Brewer's class on Thursday. And now I can't find the paper I need."

It had been approximately twenty-one hours since I saw her disappear into the subway tunnel, and I was full of conflicting emotions. Part of me was hurt because I thought she'd dumped me from the Omega team, but part was also hopeful that it was all a big misunderstanding.

"There's some theory about his work that I'm supposed to analyze, and I don't even remotely understand it," she said.

"That's amazing," I replied. "Because I thought you understood everything."

She laughed. "If you think that, then you've been fooled."

"Well, I have a theory that you might be interested in," I said.

"Is it about poetry?"

"Nope."

"I like it already," she joked.

"It's about a squad of zombies on the police force," I said with just a dash of mystery.

She stopped her search and looked right at me. "That does sound interesting."

I told her what the guys and I had come up with about

the Dead Squad. She seemed really into it and at one point even jotted down the full name of the squad. With her interest fully piqued I tried to use it as an opening to talk about Omega. I asked if she thought we might get back into action soon, and suddenly her whole attitude changed.

"I have no idea," she said. "Honestly, I've been so busy with make-up work I haven't had time to think about Dead City or Omega."

Her smile was sincere, but I knew this was a lie. After all I had seen her enter Dead City the day before. I'm sure my reaction gave me away, because she could tell something was bothering me.

"What's wrong?"

I couldn't exactly say that I had spied on her, so I decided to tell her the other thing that I wanted to talk about. (And also had me nervous.)

"It's just that my birthday is coming up and I was wondering if you'd like to celebrate with us."

She laughed. "Judging by your expression I thought it was going to be something bad. Of course I want to celebrate your birthday. I wouldn't miss it."

That response. Her eagerness, made everything else melt away. "Really?"

"Dinner and a musical, right?" she asked, referring to

my traditional celebration. "Which one are we going to see?"

"Actually, this year we're having a party," I told her. "We're going to Coney Island."

Her expression changed instantly and at first I assumed it was because she thought Coney Island was a silly way to celebrate your birthday.

"What's wrong with Coney Island?" I asked. "Too kiddie?"

She paused for a moment at a loss for words. Then she said, "No, it's just that I'll have to check with my doctors. I'm not sure I'm allowed to go on roller coasters yet."

It had never occurred to me that she might not be able to ride the rides. I apologized and she told me it was no big deal. But I still felt like a total dork.

I tried to change the subject and be a better friend. "What's the paper you're looking for?" I asked. "Let me help."

"'The Hollow Men'," she said.

"Is that one of Eliot's poems?"

She nodded. "A really depressing one."

I started sorting through a different stack of papers.

"I know there's a copy in another book," she said, getting up. "I'll try to find it in the stacks."

"I'll keep looking here," I replied.

I want to be totally honest. I was absolutely one hundred percent looking for the poem. No matter what was going on with Omega, her friendship is what mattered more. But then I noticed that her backpack was open, and I could see a piece of blue paper in the pocket where Liberty had passed her the note. It had to be the same one.

I knew it was the wrong thing to do, but I couldn't stop myself. I looked over my shoulder and saw that Natalie was still looking for the book on the shelf. I had a window of about ten to fifteen seconds.

I reached in with the tip of my fingers and pulled out the note. The message was brief and written in Omega code.

It read: 107/8/92/34 6/15/18/19

Which translates to: BhOUSe CpArK.

I wasn't sure what that meant. I wondered if it was "B House C Park." Unfortunately, I didn't have time to think it through before she came back. I quickly folded the paper and slid it into her backpack.

"Did you find it?"

I looked up and saw her right there. Then I realized she was asking about the poem.

"No," I said. "I don't see it anywhere."

"That's all right. I know it's in here." She sat down and

started flipping through the book to find the other copy.

"Why are the men 'hollow'?" I asked her, referring to the title of the poem.

"I think it has something to do with soldiers feeling empty after the end of World War One," she said. "But it makes me think of the Unlucky 13, left hollow by the explosion in the subway tunnel and wandering the underground, not really living and not really dead."

"That's pretty deep," I said. "Too bad you can't right about that for your paper."

"Comparing and contrasting the poems of T. S. Eliot with the undead of New York City," she said with a laugh. "That would really catch Ms. Brewer's attention."

"You've got a lot of work to do," I said. "I should head to lunch and let you get back to it."

"Thanks for looking," she said. "Maybe we can get together this weekend and do something fun, like pizza."

"That would be great," I replied.

After seeing her I was even more confused than I had been when the day started. I kept replaying the conversation in my head trying to analyze every word and expression as I rode the B train from Rockefeller Center to Cathedral Parkway. Ultimately, I realized I had no idea what to make of it. That's why I was headed uptown.

It took a while to figure out the coded message. I knew that "C Park" probably stood for Central Park. But I had to do an Internet search to find B House. The Blockhouse is an old fort. It's located in the northwest corner of the park right on the border of Harlem.

I read about it online as I rode the subway. It's officially known as Blockhouse #1, and two facts about it instantly caught my attention.

First of all, it was built during the Revolutionary War, interesting because the zombie we killed in the boathouse was reading a book about defending Manhattan during the Revolutionary War. If Natalie was investigating something for Omega, that might have been the reason she went there.

Secondly, not only was the fort made mostly out of Manhattan schist, but it was also built on a giant mound of schist. Schist is the rock formation that gives the undead their power. That meant for a zombie, going inside the fort would be an energy boost.

My relationship with Natalie wasn't the only thing that had me conflicted. My mother had been firm when she told me not to do anything Omega unless she got word to me. This was a close call. If I'd had to go underground, I wouldn't have done it. But the Blockhouse was not in

Dead City. It was just in Central Park; that made it okay.

At least that's what I told myself.

Even though the fort is close to the Cathedral Parkway station, it took me about fifteen minutes to find it because it's hidden in a wooded area. My guess is that hundreds of thousands of people walk by it every day with no idea that a piece of history is right there.

In addition to being hidden, the fort is also pretty boring. It's about the size of a small house and has four square walls about twelve feet high that make it look like a gray stone cube.

I wasn't sure what I was looking for, just that it had something to do with Natalie and Omega. I hoped that it would be obvious and I would be able to figure out what it was when I saw it.

I walked up a small flight of stairs to a gate in the wall. There was a chain on the gate, but when I got up close I realized that it wasn't actually locked. The chain was draped to make it look like it was, but all you had to do was reach through the bars and slide a latch to open it.

The gate made a loud creaking noise as I entered. It should have signaled something creepy, but the inside of the Blockhouse was just as boring as the out. There was a small square area surrounded by thick walls of Manhattan schist. Each wall had a pair of holes that Revolutionary soldiers could use to stick their rifles through and shoot out during an attack. There was also a flagpole right in the middle.

"Underwhelming," I muttered to myself as I tried to figure out what might have brought Natalie here.

I began to wonder if I was just wrong about the clue. Maybe "B house C Park" referred to something completely different. Maybe (hopefully) I was wrong about everything. That was when I noticed a piece of paper that had blown into the far corner.

I walked over and knelt down to check it out. It was blank on the side facing me, but when I turned it over I saw that it was a poem.

"The Hollow Men" by T. S. Eliot.

I slumped as I realized what this meant. This was where Natalie lost the poem. That meant she had come here because an Omega (Liberty) had told her to. I folded up the poem and slid it into my pocket. As I stood up, I heard the creaking of the gate closing behind me.

My first thought was that it was Natalie. I figured she had seen me digging around her backpack and followed me here to confront me about it.

"Listen, I'm sorry that I . . ."

That's as far as I got. When I turned all the way, I realized that it was most definitely *not* Natalie.

"What's that?" the man said, cupping his hand to the side of his head where his ear should be. "I couldn't hear you."

He cackled at his joke as he let the moment of surprise have its full effect. It was Officer Pell, my favorite one-eared member of the Dead Squad. He looked pleased to see me.

"Hello, Molly, what brings you here?"

The Blockhead and the Blockhouse

Pell was big and he filled the doorway, making it impossible to escape. When I didn't answer right away, he asked me again.

"I said, Hello, Molly, what brings you here?"

"Homework," I said, trying to sound calm. "I'm doing a school project on the Revolutionary War and I came here to check out the Blockhouse."

"Really? Is that the best you can do? You and I both know why you're here."

Unfortunately, I really didn't know. I was hoping to find something that made sense to me, but this was a fishing expedition. So, I decided to keep fishing.

"Okay, then why do you think I'm here?"

"You want to see where we supercharge," he said. "Watch this, I'll show you."

He smiled and pressed his back against the wall of Manhattan schist. He sucked in a deep breath of air, and it seemed like he got even bigger.

"I don't know what you're talking about," I said. "But I would like to go now."

He chuckled. "You can't go, Molly. Marek told you to stop messing around in the world of the undead. But you didn't stop, and now you're going to have to pay a penalty.

He took a step toward me and cracked his neck to both sides, loosening up for a fight.

"They tell me you're tougher than you look," he said with a grin. "I hope that's true. Because I want a little challenge."

As a place of interest, Blockhouse #1 was boring. As a place to fight a supercharged Level 2 zombie, it was a total nightmare. The four walls kept me penned in like a boxing ring. I decided that the key to my survival would be the flagpole. I tried to keep it between him and me, hoping that if he had to chase me around, he might leave an opening that let me get to the gate and escape.

"I don't know what you think Marek said, but this has nothing to do with Omega. I really am just working on a class assignment. Here, let me prove it to you." I started reciting the information I had learned during the subway ride. "Blockhouse Number One, which is the official name, was built during the Revolutionary War as part of George Washington's defense of Manhattan."

He didn't wait for more. He charged right at me, and I dropped down to the ground and did a leg sweep that surprised him and knocked him over. I jumped up and threw two quick punches into the side of his head right where his ear once was. My knuckle cracked through the scar tissue and a small trickle of black liquid dripped out.

He seemed dazed, which was the chance I was looking for. I started for the gate, but while I was sliding the lock open he grabbed me from behind. He wrapped me up in a giant bear hug and lifted me so my feet were off the ground.

"You are a better fighter than I expected," he said gleefully. "This is kind of fun. Let me demonstrate how well the supercharge works."

While he still held me in the bear hug, he walked over and pressed his back against the wall again. The schist instantly made him stronger, which kept making his grip

85

tighter and tighter. I kicked and squirmed as I felt him forcing the air out of me.

"Any last words?" he whispered into my ear.

Again with the whispering. I hate the way these zombies whisper. Although, this whisper did help me out. It let me know exactly where his head was.

"Sure," I gasped. "Heads up."

I slammed my head back into his face, which slammed his head right into the rock wall. His grip loosened and I was able to break free.

I had a sudden brainstorm. When I was studying jeet kune do, I went to a martial arts demonstration and a man showed us how to walk up a pole. It's tricky but possible. You keep your arms straight as you grab it, and then you tuck your legs up toward your chest and sort of walk up.

I had never actually done it, but I decided this might be the time to try. Pell was giving himself a little recharge on the wall by the gate, which gave me just enough time.

He had no idea what I was doing until it was too late. By the time he got to the pole, I was up beyond his reach. Even so, I climbed a little bit higher just to be safe. He jumped a couple times but couldn't touch me. Still, it was obvious he felt in control of the situation.

"What's your plan, Molly?" he taunted from below.

"Your arms are going to get tired really soon. And when they do, you're going to have to come down."

He had a point there, but climbing the pole gave me a chance to think. I was high enough that I could see over the wall. If someone walked by I could yell for help. The only problem was that out here in the wooded section of the park there was only a small path nearby. I didn't see anybody walking on it.

Then it dawned on me. I could see over the wall, but he couldn't. He had no idea what was out there. That's when I crossed my fingers and hoped that Beth hadn't gotten all of the family's acting genes.

"Hello," I called to a make-believe rescuer. "Hello! I need your help."

Suddenly, Pell was concerned, although he tried to cover it.

"No one's going to help you, Molly. Remember I'm a police officer."

I looked down. "Yeah. But so is he, and he's going to wonder why you're harassing a twelve-year-old girl. He might even wonder what someone in the Departmental Emergency Action Deployment Squad is doing in Blockhouse Number One. It's not exactly your beat, is it?"

Now he was really nervous. "Molly, stop it."

"Officer, I need your help!" I called out. "Yes. Yes. I'm over here. Thank you so much."

There was something about the thought of an outside police officer getting involved that worried Pell, which is exactly what I was hoping for. He frantically tried to climb up the flagpole to grab at my feet. And, while he didn't get very high, he got just high enough for the next step in my plan.

I didn't need my dad to take me to a firehouse in order to slide down a pole. I loosened my grip and slid down right into him. I jammed my heel into the top of his head and we both slammed hard into the rocky ground, although he broke my fall and I landed on top of him.

His walkie-talkie fell off of his belt and I picked it up and used it like a weapon, slamming it against his head a few times. There was more black liquid dripping out.

He was unconscious, but I don't think he was dead. I didn't care. I just wanted to get out of there. I charged through the gate and sprinted through the park as fast as I could. I didn't stop to catch my breath until I was on the subway heading home.

I plopped down into the seat and breathed a sigh of relief. Then I heard a voice crackle and say.

"Pell. Pell."

It startled me until I realized that it was coming over the walkie-talkie. I hasn't noticed that I still had it.

"Someone better let the chief know that Pell's not responding," the voice said. "We're going to go look for him."

It occurred to me that a walkie-talkie that could listen to transmissions of the Dead Squad might come in handy. But for the moment, I didn't need to attract any attention. I turned it off and slipped it into my backpack.

There was no one in the apartment when I got home, which was a relief. I was messy from the fight and wanted to clean up before my father or sister saw me.

I had a couple of small cuts and bruises, and there was some of the black fluid on me. I was careful to make sure none of it got near the cuts, and then after I got it all off, I dug out some rubbing alcohol and cleaned it some more.

Finally I staggered into my room and lay down on the bed. I felt the crinkle of paper in my back pocket, and I reached in and pulled out the poem that I had found in the Blockhouse. I scanned it for a moment, and the last two lines caught my eye.

This is the way the world ends
Not with a bang but a whimper.

I thought about the fact that my world almost ended with a whimper in the Blockhouse. I was lucky to have made it out in one piece. It was so stupid. I wasn't even doing anything for Omega; I was just snooping around trying to figure out what was up with Natalie. I made two decisions.

Decision one: I would actually do what my mother said and avoid anything remotely related to Omega. I couldn't risk getting hurt and, even worse, I couldn't risk starting the all-out war that Marek had threatened. Those two words he said, "undead army," still gave me panic attacks.

Decision two: I should give up trying to figure out what was going on with Natalie. If and when she felt like she could tell me, she would. Until then, I was determined to be the best friend that I could possibly be.

I felt good about both decisions and was about to take a nap when I saw that another envelope had arrived. Either Beth or my dad had left it on my dresser.

Like the first one, it was addressed to me with no name above the return address. I opened it and it contained a folded map of Manhattan. On the front was a picture of George Washington.

I unfolded it and saw that the map was made for visitors by the National Park Service and that it laid out a tour of places with some connection to the first President.

Just as there was with the first envelope, there was a piece of paper with a single sentence written in block letters with a blue felt tip pen. It said:

RESERVE A PLACE IN HISTORY

Thirteen Candles

The only reason I'm letting you get away with that out-fit is because it's your birthday."

Beth was talking. But she was also texting. In fact, she was texting so intently I assumed she was just saying the words as she typed them, like movie subtitles but in reverse. That's why I didn't respond at first.

"Are you talking to me?"

"No, I'm talking to the total stranger standing over there in white shorts, black socks, and red sandals," she said, shaking her head as she continued texting. "Of course I'm talking to you. It is *your* birthday, isn't it?"

We were in Brooklyn at the corner of Stillwell and Surf Avenues. I have no idea how she could simultaneously talk, text, and keep track of peripheral fashion violations, but I was impressed. Unlike the man in the socks and sandals, however, I had actually put some thought and consideration into what I was wearing.

"What's wrong with my outfit?" I asked.

"You mean other than the fact that those shorts and that top belong to me?"

Busted again. I thought I could get away with it because I found them in that sad box of clothes she hangs onto in case old trends come back into fashion.

"I figured when they go into the box, it means . . ."

She looked up from the phone for the first time in our conversation. "Just because I haven't worn them in a while, doesn't mean they're forgotten."

"I just wanted to look . . ."

". . . like a teenager," she said, completing my thought. "I get it. That's why I'm classifying it as borrowing and not theft. No penalty."

"Really?" I said, grateful. "Does that mean you might let me borrow them *permanently*?"

She considered this for a second and then shook her head.

"Not after seeing how good they look together," she said. "I never wore them as an outfit. I think they may get promoted back into the closet. Not for school, but for weekend wear."

As much as I wanted to keep the clothes, I kind of loved the fact that Beth was willing to wear an outfit that I had put together. Mark that as a first.

"You know, if you're interested," she continued, "we can look for some new clothes during spring break. I know a couple places in the Village where you can get something cute without spending too much money."

"That would be incredible," I said. "I absolutely would love to do that."

Even though she immediately went back to texting, I considered it a total teenage sister bonding moment.

I had only been thirteen for half a day, but so far it was great. It began when my dad surprised me with my favorite breakfast—bacon pancakes. (That's right, they're pancakes with bacon mixed right into the batter so you get both tastes in every bite!) Now Beth was volunteering to take me to Greenwich Village to find cool clothes. And my friends and I were about to spend the day having fun at Coney Island.

"I've got wristbands and tickets," my dad said as he

approached, and waved them in the air for me to see. "The wristbands give you unlimited rides on everything but the Cyclone. And the tickets are for the Cyclone. It's going to be great. I'm so glad I thought of this."

My sister didn't say a word. She just raised her eyebrow and he instantly corrected himself.

"I mean I'm so glad Beth thought of this."

She smiled and continued texting.

He gave me a map of all the rides and attractions and I started plotting the day's activities. The plan was for Alex, Grayson, Natalie, and I to ride the rides for a few hours while Dad went back home and did his miracle work in the kitchen to make dinner and a cake. Beth was going to hang out nearby with some friends on the beach in case we needed anything. The thought that we were going to be on our own made thirteen feel even cooler.

A few minutes later Alex and Grayson arrived.

Alex inhaled deeply before letting out an exaggerated breath. "Is that the best smell in the world, or what?"

"The salt air coming off the ocean?" asked Grayson.

Alex shook his head.

"Salt air's nice, but seventy-one percent of the earth is covered by ocean," he said. "No, I was referring to the singular place on the planet where you can breathe in the awesomeness that is the original Nathan's Famous hot dogs."

The "famous" in Nathan's Famous is legit. It's legendary. It's a hot dog stand that fills an entire block and hosts the world championships of hot dog eating every Fourth of July. We were standing right in front of it.

"Happy birthday," Alex said as he handed me a present.

Even though it was wrapped, the shape and feel kind of gave it away.

"I'm guessing . . . baseball cap."

"That's a good guess," he said. "But do you know the team?"

For this there could only be one answer. "It better be the Yankees."

He shrugged his shoulders. "Maybe it is. Maybe it isn't. You'll have to unwrap it to know for sure."

With my lack of birthday party experience, I wasn't sure if I was supposed to open it then or wait until later. I looked to Dad for guidance.

"Go ahead and open it," he said. "I want to know which team it is too."

I tore it open expecting to see the classic Yankee design of navy hat with an *NY* logo, but instead it was a lighter blue and had a white *B* on the front. I didn't recognize it.

"The Dodgers," said Alex.

"Then why is there a *B*?" I asked. "The Dodgers play in Los Angeles."

"They do now," he said. "But they used to play right here in Brooklyn. And it was on this date, your birthday, in 1947, that Jackie Robinson became the first African American to play in the major leagues. He's my hero and was incredibly brave . . . just like you."

Every now and then I'm reminded that Alex is totally awesome and thoughtful. I slipped on the cap and it fit perfectly.

"I love it."

"And this is from me," Grayson said as he handed me a card.

I opened it to find a pair of tickets to the new space show at the Hayden Planetarium.

"Greatness!" I exclaimed. "I want to see this so bad."

Like I said, thirteen was off to a great start. Which is not to say that everything went exactly as I hoped. A couple minutes later I got a call from Natalie that dampened the mood a little. I knew there was a chance she wasn't going to come, but in my heart I thought she'd make it.

I was wrong.

She called and apologized, saying that her doctors and

parents wouldn't let her. I understood, but I was still disappointed. I also felt bad because my dad bought four wristbands and it turned out we only needed three.

"Do you think you can get your money back?" I asked him. "For the extra wristband?"

"What extra wristband?" Beth said, taking the last one from my father.

"I thought you were going to meet your friends at the beach?" I asked.

Beth whipped out her phone and sent a lightning quick text.

"Done," she said. "Now, are we going to have fun or are we just going to stand around and talk?"

It's amazing how much of a difference one person can make. If it had only been Alex, Grayson, and me, I don't think it would have felt as much like a party. But four was the perfect number. When we went on the go-karts, we raced boys against the girls. When we rode the roller coasters, no one ended up sitting alone. It was also cool because it was the first time Alex and Grayson got to hang out with her.

She told them about her plans to work at drama camp that summer and amazed them with her ability to do different accents. She could switch from Bronx to

Queens to Long Island in the middle of a sentence.

The Cyclone was fun for everyone else, but with my dislike for heights I'm not really a big roller coaster fan. I was much more into the bumper cars because they have lots of excitement but stay close to the ground. And also because Beth turned it into a challenge.

"I have a secret mission for you two," she said to the boys, using an exaggerated Eastern European accent. "Do everything you can to make sure Molly does not make it all the way around the track."

"Hey!" I complained. "That's not fair."

"Let me finish," she said, turning to me. "If you can complete an entire lap, you can keep the clothes."

"That's a deal," I said, giddy with excitement. "Challenge accepted."

I hopped into the car and strapped on my safety belt nice and tight. The cars sparked to life and the battle began. The three of them chased me in circles, slammed me with their bumpers, and hounded me all around.

They had me pretty good until I realized that I should stop thinking of it as an amusement park ride and instead consider it a physics experiment. Bumper cars are a perfect demonstration of Newton's laws of motion. Rather than go head to head, where I was losing out, I decided to change direction ever so slightly, which diverted their energy and let me escape from the pack.

It was a bold and exciting move but I soon learned that Newton's laws of motion are nothing compared to Beth's law's of fashion. She was not about to let me get those clothes, and somehow she managed to drive backward and trap me in a corner until the time ran out.

"You put up a good fight," she said as she reached down to help me out of the car. "You even worked up a sweat."

For a second I thought she was going to give me the outfit anyway.

"Make sure you take the clothes to the dry cleaners before you put them back in my closet."

I was so busy having a great time that I didn't really think much about Natalie being a no-show. At least not until after dinner and cake. (The cake, by the way, was out-of-control amazing. It had cream cheese frosting and a layer of raspberry filling. I thought Alex was going to faint when he took his first taste.) I know she had a good excuse, but it still made me wonder about our friendship. And since I was now a teenager, I decided the mature thing would be to talk to her about it. That's why I headed over to see her the next morning.

I spent the entire subway ride trying to come up

with the right way to say what I was feeling.

Natalie, I want to talk to you about our friendship.

Natalie, I want you to be honest with me.

Natalie, is there something you want to tell me?

Each line sounded more and more ridiculous. I didn't want to be emotional or dramatic, just honest. By the time I stepped into the elevator, I realized I was getting worked up and needed to relax. Luckily, I had all the way to the twelfth floor to take a couple of deep breaths and calm down. Rather than blurt it out, I decided the best approach would be to say that I was in the neighborhood and wanted to stop by to see how she was doing. I'd let the conversation flow from there.

I knocked on the door and panicked as I realized that it was a terrible excuse. Her neighborhood was nowhere near mine. It didn't make sense for me to be there. I was still trying to come up with a better reason when the door opened.

"Can I help you?"

I went to talk and then I saw that it wasn't Natalie or her mother. It was some random woman who I'd never seen before. I wondered if she was one of the doctors working with her.

"I'm sorry," I said confused. "I'm looking for my friend Natalie Allen."

The woman smiled. "The Allens are downstairs in apartment 2B."

"Sorry, I totally forgot."

In my moment of full diva drama I'd forgotten that Natalie and her family had moved downstairs. Now I had another elevator ride to come up with a better excuse. But as I started down toward the second floor I realized something. Natalie and her family had moved so their apartment could be renovated. But it wasn't being renovated. An entirely different family was living in it.

That made no sense.

Why had a temporary move become permanent? Why would Natalie's family move ten flights downstairs to a less exclusive apartment? That didn't seem like them at all. Her parents were so proud of their view of Central Park. They also seemed to have an endless supply of money and loved to show it off.

When I got to the second floor, I knocked on the door for 2B. And it was then, while I was waiting for someone to answer, that I figured out a possible answer to my question. It was an answer that was totally ridiculous, yet somehow explained everything that had been going on with Natalie lately. It was an answer that took my breath away.

She had moved from the twelfth floor to the second.

She had gone down into Dead City with someone I had never seen before. She'd gone into the Blockhouse where the undead go to recharge. She said she wanted to come to my party when she thought it was going to be dinner and a musical in Manhattan, but canceled when she learned it was Coney Island in Brooklyn.

What if none of this had anything to do with our friendship or Omega and instead was all about Manhattan schist?

What if Natalie was undead?

The Scientific Method as Applied to Potential Zombies

I t would have been nice if I'd had this brainstorm *before* I knocked on the door. That would have given me a chance to think through my theory and figure out if it was a stroke of genius or just plain crazy. But that's not what happened. Instead this was the order of events as they unfolded in the hallway outside of Apartment 2B: Knock first. Crazy idea second. Awkward moment when Natalie opens the door and I stand there with my mouth wide open third.

"Hey, Molls, what's up?"

I was pretty sure I was making some sort of "I just

figured out you might be a zombie but don't want you to know" face, so I tried to fake a smile.

"Nothing much," I said as casually as I could. "I was just in the neighborhood and wanted to see how you're doing."

"I'm good, thanks," she said. "Come on in."

We walked into the front room, and as we sat down she asked, "What were you doing on the Upper West Side on a Sunday morning?"

I'm a lousy liar and normally freeze at these moments, but I actually came up with a believable excuse. "I'm going to see the new space show at the Hayden Planetarium," I explained. "Grayson got me tickets for my birthday."

The planetarium is part of the Museum of Natural History and is a short walk from Natalie's building.

"My parents went to the grand opening," she replied. "They said it was amazing."

And just as suddenly as it came, my newfound ability to think fast and say clever things disappeared. I couldn't think of any follow-up. My mind just kept racing as I looked at her, trying to figure out if it was possibly true. Luckily, after a brief but awkward silence, she took over the conversation.

"Listen, I want to apologize about yesterday."

With my mind still scrambling through variations of her potential state of undeadness, I had no idea what she was talking about.

"What about yesterday?" I asked.

"Missing your birthday," she said. "I'm so sorry I didn't make it to your party. I really wanted to go."

Two minutes earlier this subject had been so important I had to rush over to confront her about it. It was the topic I wanted to analyze in minute detail so we could figure out what it said about our friendship. Now it was so insignificant I was able to resolve it in two sentences.

"I'm sorry you missed it too. We had a lot of fun."

One problem was over, but the other was just beginning. The thought that she might be undead may have been a crazy idea, but that didn't mean it was wrong. I had to figure out the truth.

"I just remembered something," she said, getting up. "I've got a birthday present for you. I was going to bring it to school tomorrow, but now you don't have to wait. It's in my room."

I remembered that when we came over before, she said her room was filled with medical equipment. I wondered if seeing it might help me figure things out. I stood up to go with her.

"Nope, you wait here," she said. "I've got to wrap it."

"You don't need to go to all that trouble," I said.

She tapped the couch for me to sit back down. "It will only take a second."

The whole thing was surreal. My mouth was having a normal conversation while my brain was spinning wild conspiracy theories about her possible zombie conversion. When she went to her room, it gave me a moment to think things through. Faced with an unproven theory, I did exactly what they taught us to do at MIST. I employed the scientific method:

Observation
Hypothesis
Test
Analysis

My observations went back to the fight on New Year's Eve. First I considered the two ways a person can become undead. One is when the dead flesh of a zombie contaminates an open wound, leading to infection and disease. (This is what happened to my mother.) The other is when someone dies suddenly in an underground area where Manhattan schist is plentiful. (This is what happened to the Unlucky

13 in the subway tunnel explosion that started all of this.)

Either scenario could have happened to Natalie. Her fight with Edmund was intense, and I remember that she was bleeding when it was over. She could have easily been infected. Also, even though we were in an abandoned pressroom, we were underground and there was schist all around us.

The more important observations, though, dealt with her behavior after getting hurt. Going underground, visiting Blockhouse #1, and changing apartments from the twelfth to the second floor were all consistent with someone trying to be closer to Manhattan schist.

I also couldn't think of a single time she'd left Manhattan since she got hurt. A trip to see her grandparents in New Jersey was canceled, and once when we were going to have lunch at Grayson's in Brooklyn, Nat had a sudden craving for Shake Shack and we ended up getting burgers in Madison Square Park instead.

None of this was conclusive, but it was strong enough for me to build my hypothesis, which was that Natalie had been turned into a zombie during or soon after our fight on New Year's Eve. Since I was not about to poke her and see if purple goo oozed out of her skin, my test would have to be more creative.

"I hope you like it," she said when she came back into

the room, holding my present. "When I saw it I instantly thought of you."

She handed me a small, perfectly wrapped box. I felt guilty taking it, considering what I was thinking about her at the moment. I felt even guiltier because when she handed it to me, I pressed my fingers against her hand, trying to gauge her body temperature.

"I'm sure I'll love it," I said.

I unwrapped it and opened the lid to reveal a silver bracelet with a charm on it. I held it up to get a good look at it. The charm looked like an old-style New York subway token.

"Remember the Omega necklace you wore on the first day of school?" she asked.

"You mean the one that made an evil zombie attack me in the subway station?" (I worried that I shouldn't have used the Z word, but it didn't seem to bother her.)

"That's the one," she said. "I thought this might be a good substitute. You can wear it, but the bad guys won't know that it has anything to do with Omega."

I put it on my wrist. "I love it, Natalie. It's perfect."

She smiled and added, "Now we're twins."

She held up her wrist so that I could see she was wearing an identical bracelet. I was truly touched by the sentiment.

I reminded myself that Natalie was my friend, and whether or not she was undead shouldn't matter. After all, my own mother was undead. I thought back to that day when I was attacked. Natalie was the one who saved me.

I looked at her for a moment and decided that I should at least be straight with her. "Can I ask you something?"

"Of course," she said.

"Are you . . . ?" It just hung there while I tried to think of a way to say it.

"Am I what?"

I realized I couldn't just blurt out *Are you a zombie?* If I was wrong she'd never forgive me, and if I was right, well, she probably wouldn't forgive me for that, either.

". . . busy this afternoon? I feel bad about having a party that you couldn't come to, so I thought you might like to catch the show with me at the planetarium. Grayson gave me two tickets."

"Actually," she said, "I am busy. My parents and I are having lunch at the club."

This was fantastic news. Natalie's family belongs to a country club where they like to go on the weekends so her parents can play golf and she can ride her horse, Coperni-cus. The reason this was such great news is because the club is on Long Island. If she could go there, it meant that she wasn't undead after all. I considered this to be a test result that proved my hypothesis wrong.

"That sounds great," I said. "Are you going to ride Copernicus when you're there? Or do your doctors want you to wait longer?"

"Not that club," she said. "We're going to my dad's university club. There's some sort of special Sunday brunch thing."

I remembered that her dad went to Yale, but I had no idea where the club was located. "Where's that?"

"Midtown," she said. "Right by Grand Central."

"Oh," I said, trying to hide my disappointment. She wasn't leaving Manhattan, but that didn't mean she couldn't. My test was still inconclusive, so I decided to push just a little bit more.

"When are you going to go visit Copernicus next?" I asked.

She looked pained by the question and sighed before answering. "Actually, we ended up selling him. It's expensive to take care of a horse, and with my injuries and all the schoolwork, I've had less and less time to ride."

Natalie loved Copernicus more than anything. The only way she'd let her parents sell him was if there was no way for her to ride him again. I was heartbroken for her.

"I'm so sorry to hear that."

It took all my concentration to keep from crying. We were quiet for what seemed like a minute, and I wondered if she was going to just break down and tell me on the spot. But she didn't say anything.

"I really love the bracelet," I said as I stood up to leave. "I better get over to the planetarium. The show starts soon."

"Thanks for stopping by," she said.

"Thanks for the present."

Just like I had when I visited her right after she got out of the hospital, I hugged Natalie at the door. Only this time, there was nothing awkward about it. I knew she needed friends now more than ever.

I was in a daze when I got to the sidewalk. At first I headed for the planetarium. Even though it started out as a phony excuse, I thought the show might cheer me up. But, as I got closer, I realized I wasn't in the mood. I was too sad.

Instead I wandered through Central Park and thought about everything Natalie must have been going through. Technically, my test results didn't prove my hypothesis, but I had no doubt.

My walk ended up right at the Delacorte Clock and the entrance to the Central Park Zoo. One of the great things about the zoo is that even if you don't go in, the walkway through the park is close enough for you to see some of the animal exhibits.

I stopped and watched the sea lions playing in their pool as my mind ran through everything. I wondered if my mother knew about Natalie. I wished that I could talk to her about it. I turned around and stared at the clock.

My mom and I couldn't use it anymore as a secret message board. We'd lost that the moment Marek Blackwell discovered it.

When the clock struck noon, the animal sculptures came to life and started playing "Row, Row, Row Your Boat," just like they had that last time I saw her.

I thought back to that day and one question kept going through my mind. *How in the world did Marek find out that my mother and I used the clock?*

After all, no one else knew about it.

That's when I got a sick feeling in my stomach. I realized there was one other person who knew about it.

Natalie. She had discovered it before Christmas.

Suddenly I remembered that on the day that Marek surprised my mother and me, Natalie had asked me about the clock and said I should I go check for a message.

The sick feeling got worse.

If it was possible that Natalie was a zombie, then it was possible that she was a Level 2. That would mean she'd have no conscience or sense of right and wrong.

I sat down on a bench and slumped under the weight of it all. I looked at the charm on my bracelet as it glistened in the sunlight.

Was it possible that the person who gave me one of the sweetest gifts I'd ever received was also the person giving Marek Blackwell inside information about the Omegas?

My second day as a teenager was nowhere near as good as my first.

Hogwarts in Harlem

M olly, is something wrong?"

Grayson was probably wondering why I was just staring blankly at my open locker.

"No," I said as I snapped out of it and shut the door. "Just tired. I didn't sleep well last night."

That was true, I hadn't slept well. In fact, I hadn't slept well all week. But that's not why I was dazed and confused. The lack of sleep hadn't put me in the funk, but the funk was keeping me up at night. It had been that way ever since I first suspected Natalie might be undead. I'd tossed and turned each night as I tried to figure out what I should do.

I thought about telling Alex and Grayson, but decided against it. There'd be no way to undo the damage if I was wrong.

"Are you sure that's all it is?" he said.

I smiled and lied. "I'm sure."

Before he could dig any deeper, the warning bell rang, signaling one minute until the next period began. We said our quick see-you-laters and hurried down the hall in opposite directions. I was just about to go into my English class, when I noticed a flyer posted next to the door.

According to the flyer, a professor at City College was going to give an "in-depth visual presentation about the birds of Central Park." That's a nice way of saying he was going to spend two hours showing pictures of mute swans, downy woodpeckers, and who knows how many of the other more than two hundred species that inhabit the park. I couldn't imagine a single one of my classmates wanting to sit through it.

It sounded boring to *me*, and I'm actually interested in birds. My mother convinced me to join the New York Audubon Society's Junior Birder program when I was eight, and as a result I can now identify most of the birds that are common in the city. I even know the difference between red-tailed hawks, which like to nest along Fifth Avenue, and red-shouldered hawks, which sometimes fly over the park but won't nest there.

Across the top of the flyer were pictures of five birds: a warbler, a swan, a starling, a heron, and a pigeon. It was the pigeon that caught my attention. New York is overrun with pigeons. They're everywhere. But the pigeon in this picture isn't the type you'd find in Central Park. It's the kind you'd find in Central Africa. It's even called the African pigeon.

If Professor Michael Stimola, PhD was actually a leading bird expert, how could he possibly make that mistake? I was trying to figure this out when Ms. White tapped me on the shoulder.

"Molly, will you be joining us?" she asked.

I shrugged. "Probably not. It sounds really boring."

When I saw her expression, I realized she wasn't talking about the lecture. The tardy bell had rung and she was about to close the door and start class.

"Wait a second, you meant English class, didn't you?"

"That is why they pay me."

"Of course I'll be joining you," I said sheepishly. "And, for the record, I'm sure it won't be boring at all."

"Better answer," she replied.

We were discussing *A Wrinkle in Time*, a science-fiction

book about a girl who travels through time, searching for her lost father.

It's my favorite of the books we've read for class. I especially like Meg, the main character. She's geeky, socially awkward, and desperate to reunite with a missing parent. In other words, she's a lot like the girl I see in the mirror every morning. Despite this connection, I was having trouble staying interested in the class discussion.

The mistake on the flyer just bothered me too much. So rather than take notes that might come in handy on our upcoming test, I doodled the names of the five birds down the side of my paper and stared at them.

Warbler
Swan
Starling
Heron
Pigeon

I'll admit that I may have been making a big deal over nothing more than a simple mistake. I have been known to do that. I even have a history of overreacting to geographically misplaced birds.

My dad loves to tell the story about when I was six years old and we visited a neighborhood that was decorated for Christmas. We were walking through a yard that was made to look like Santa's workshop at the North Pole. I started laughing because there were giant plastic penguins in Santa hats. I didn't mean to be rude. I thought it was a joke and that you were supposed to laugh, because *everybody* knows that penguins only live in the Southern Hemisphere, not the Northern.

Well, apparently not everybody.

It turns out it wasn't a joke and the people who lived there were offended. I apologized and later my parents explained that you don't always need to point out mistakes that others make. I usually do a good job of remembering that, but this was different. This was a bird expert giving a lecture at a top college.

I kept doodling and filled in the formal names of the different species.

orange-crowned warbler
mute swan
European starling
great blue heron
African pigeon

It took me about thirty seconds to see it, but when I did I let out a hoot that made Ms. White stop in the middle of a sentence.

"Is there something you'd like to add to the discussion, Molly?"

All eyes trained on me. "Just . . . that it's a . . . really good book."

"That's all?" she asked, shooting me a look.

I nodded. "Pretty much."

"Let's hope your book report goes into greater detail."

"It will," I promised.

The instant she went back to talking, I looked back at my paper and smiled. My funk was over and my heart was racing as I drew a circle around the first letter in each name like I was playing a word search puzzle.

It spelled out "Omega."

It had to be a message from my mother. She's the one who made me join the Junior Birders, and she'd know I'd be the only student who could decipher the code. I don't know how she got it posted next to the door to my English class, but I was certain she was trying to tell me something. I wanted to get a hall pass so I could go back and look for more clues on the flyer, but I figured I'd already caused enough distractions in this class for one day, so I waited until the bell rang.

The lecture was scheduled for Saturday at noon. I couldn't wait to tell the others. But then I noticed something else on the bottom. There were pictures of five more birds: an albatross, a loon, an owl, a nighthawk, and an eagle. Using the same coding method, I realized the first letter of each spelled out the word "alone."

I guess my mother didn't want the others to come with me. Maybe it had to do with Natalie. If Mom knew she was undead, she might not trust her to be part of the team.

That Saturday I took the train to 137th Street and walked the last couple blocks to the CCNY campus. (CCNY is the abbreviation for City College of New York.) Part of me felt like the time travelers in the book I was reading, because one moment I was walking in modern day New York, and then I passed through a giant archway and found myself in a secret world of tree-lined paths and gothic buildings. It was like Hogwarts in Harlem.

The campus was built at the same time many of the city's subway tunnels were being dug, and as a result the buildings were constructed out of the leftover rock. That's right, it's an entire campus made out of Manhattan schist. The first thought that went through my mind was that Natalie should think about going to college here where she would be surrounded by it. (That is, if Natalie turned out to be a zombie, which I was still hoping wouldn't be the case.)

The largest building on campus is Shepard Hall, which looks like a medieval cathedral. It's even decorated with gargoyles and grotesque statues on the walls and archways. The presentation was scheduled for a lecture hall on the third floor, and even though I got there right before the noon start time, the room was entirely empty. Apparently, I wasn't the only person who thought it sounded boring.

I took a seat in the middle of the third row. Moments later a giant bell in the building's main tower struck twelve times, and I heard someone enter the room behind me and close the door.

I turned to see a man with a friendly face and a close-cropped white beard. He wore jeans and a sport coat along with a black beret that gave him the air of professorial creativity.

"Hello, I'm Dr. Stimola, and I'd like to welcome you to the City College Lecture Series," he announced, starting right up while he was still in the back of the room fumbling with some equipment. "I'm an ornithologist, and if any of you are unfamiliar with that term, 'ornithology,' it's the study of birds."

Any of us? I looked around the room to make sure that I was still the only other person there. I was.

The lights dimmed, and a picture of a green-headed duck was projected on a screen at the front of the room.

"I'd like for us to get started with some of the more common birds in the park," he continued. "This is *Anas platyrhynchos*, better known as the Mallard or the wild duck."

I was totally confused. He was acting like there was a room full of students, and I was worried that I'd misread the clue and was now stuck in a two-hour lecture about birds given by a man even more socially awkward than I am. He continued to drone on about the mallard, and I was trying to figure out a way to excuse myself when a tap on my shoulder startled me. I almost leapt out of my seat.

"Shh," he whispered.

I turned to see that it was the professor. At some point when he was setting up, he'd stopped talking and was instead playing a prerecorded version of the lecture.

"Hello, Molly. Your mother wanted me to tell you that the Gingerbread House was entirely your fault."

I was totally confused for a moment, and then I made the connection. Once, when we were on a vacation to Pennsylvania, I picked a place for us to eat lunch. It was called the Gingerbread House and it was terrible. Everyone blamed me for the lousy meal and I was banned from picking restaurants from that point on. I thought this was completely unfair for one simple reason.

"I was five years old," I said, shaking my head in disbelief.

"You know who else was five years old?" he asked.

I thought about it for a moment and answered, "Mozart, when he started composing music."

It was a running joke between my mother and me. She said that if Mozart was old enough to compose music, I was old enough to take the blame for the Gingerbread House.

"Is that why you wanted me to come here today?" I asked. "So you could blame me for something I did when I was five?"

"No," he said with a nice smile. "I'm blaming you so you'll know that your mother sent me and that it's safe to come with me."

"Come with you where?" I asked.

"I'll let her tell you when we get there."

"I'm going to see my Mom?"

He nodded. "And she's not alone."

The Catacombs of CCNY

T he presentation continued on autopilot as the pre-recorded lecture played and pictures of birds were projected onto the screen. Meanwhile, I followed the professor into an office that was located at the front of the lecture hall, and he signaled me to be quiet until we were inside and he shut the door.

"We've got a lot to do and not a lot of time," he added. "So please give me your backpack."

"Why?" I asked as I handed it to him.

"I'm pretty sure that's where they hid it."

"Hid what?" I asked.

"It's easier if I just show it to you," he said as he started digging through my backpack. The shelves in his office were filled with books about birds and beautiful black-and-white photos of the city.

"Cool shot," I said, admiring one of the Chrysler Building.

"Thanks," he said as he kept digging. "I started off taking pictures of birds, and then I became fascinated with the city and its architecture."

I already knew that I liked him.

We could hear the lecture continue in the other room. "The northern cardinal has a wingspan of twenty-five to thirty-one centimeters . . ."

"By the way, my real class discussions are much more interesting. This one was intentionally designed to keep people away."

I laughed. "It seems to have worked, but why go to all of the trouble of having a recording."

"I locked the door and put up a 'do not interrupt' sign, but just in case any of Marek's men come and put an ear up to the door, I want them to overhear the most boring lecture in the history of mankind. It should get rid of them pretty quickly."

"I don't think anyone was following me," I said. "I was careful."

"They don't need to follow you," he said as he turned a pocket of my backpack inside out. "They have this." He pointed at a small silver and glass capsule that was hidden in one of the seams.

"What is that?" I asked in total disbelief.

"An RFID chip," he explained. "Radio-frequency identification. It's what they put in pet collars so you can find your dog if he gets lost."

I was stunned. "Does that mean they've been listening to me?"

"No, it's not a microphone," he said. "They can't hear anything. They can't even track where you are all the time. That would burn through the battery too quickly. But whenever they want to find you, they can send a signal and they'll get a reply on a map."

"I can't believe it," I said. "So you're destroying it?"

"I'm doing no such thing," he said. "If we destroyed it they'd know you found it and they'd come up with another way to track you. Let them think they've got you fooled. Just don't ever forget it's in there. For now, though, we're going to leave it behind."

He placed the backpack on his desk.

"If they look for you in the next two hours, they'll think you're here," he said. "Which is good, because we don't want them to know where you'll really be."

He opened a closet door and pulled on a shelf to reveal a hidden door and a spiral staircase running through the building.

"Cool, isn't it?" he said when he saw my reaction.

"Amazing," I said. "Where's it go?"

He flashed a big smile. "Have you ever heard of the catacombs of CCNY?"

"No?"

"That's good," he said as he started making his way down the stairs. "We like to keep them a secret."

The staircase was the color of tarnished brass and seemed to descend forever as I followed the professor all the way to the bottom. There we reached a long narrow tunnel cut into the Manhattan schist. The walls were close enough so I could reach out and touch both sides at the same time. It's a good thing I'm only scared of heights, because if I were claustrophobic I might have passed out.

"Stay close," he said as he motioned for me to follow. "The lighting's bad and you do not want to get lost down here."

"You got that right," I replied as I hurried to keep up with his pace.

As far as freaky scary elements go, the tunnel had plenty. The lights were dim and spaced far enough apart so that you had to walk through pools of total darkness every twenty feet or so. But that was nothing compared to the otherworldly rumbling and hissing noises that passed overhead at regular intervals. The professor assured me that although they sounded like a phantom army of disembodied souls coming to attack us, they were actually caused by something much more mundane.

"Steam pipes," he explained, pointing toward the ceiling. "They heat up the buildings on campus."

"They do a good job on the tunnel, too," I replied, wiping the sweat from my forehead. "It's like a rainforest down here."

Soon we veered into a mazelike series of brick passageways. I tried to memorize the turns but quickly lost track. I was hopelessly confused by the time we dead-ended into a wall with three large pipes running along it. Each pipe had a valve control that looked like a steering wheel, and hanging from each wheel was a metal sign reading, CAUTION—EXTREME HEAT.

"This is where it gets tricky," he said ominously.

I nodded back toward the path we just traveled. "You mean all of that wasn't tricky?"

He laughed.

"Okay, this is where it gets *trickier*. Two of these are release valves. If you turn either one, it will let off a steam blast that can be as hot as four hundred degrees."

"So I'm guessing we don't want to turn those," I said.

"No we don't," he said. "But if any of Marek's men ever made it this far and they were trying to locate what I'm about to show you . . ."

"They wouldn't be able to tell which one wasn't real," I said, finishing his sentence. "Because they can't feel the heat on the pipes."

"That's right," he said. "You're good at this."

He turned the middle wheel and I reflexively braced for a blast of steam, but instead there was only the sound of a door opening. The wheel was actually a giant door-knob, and when he pushed on it, that portion of the brick wall opened to reveal a large laboratory.

"Welcome to the *Workshop*," he said with dramatic flair.

The lab looked like something out of an old Franken-stein movie but modern. It was as if someone had taken the scientific equipment of a century ago and partially updated it so that it seemed both antique and new at the same time. Across the room two scientists were working on an experiment. They wore thick white lab coats and aviator-style safety goggles with blue lenses. It took me a moment to recognize that one of them was my mother.

"Molly!" she said as she took off the goggles. "I knew you'd figure out the clue."

She hurried over and wrapped me up in a huge hug. For a moment I closed my eyes and ignored our surroundings. It was just my mother and me, and I needed this more than anything.

"What is this place?" I asked, admiring at it all.

"We call it the Workshop," she said. "It's where we do research and planning. I guess you could say that it's Omega's headquarters."

As her lab partner approached and took off his goggles, I realized that it was Dr. Gootman, or rather the man I knew as Dr. Gootman when he was principal at MIST. I later learned he was actually Milton Blackwell, one of the so-called Unlucky 13, the original zombies who became undead when an explosion killed the crew digging the city's first subway tunnel. He founded Omega to keep his brother Marek and the other eleven from getting out of control.

"Hi, Dr. Gootman . . . or should I call you Mr. Blackwell . . . or is it Dr. Blackwell?"

"Let's go with Milton."

"Okay," I said, feeling both cool and awkward at the same time. "Milton."

"You're the first one to arrive," Mom said. "So why don't I show you around while we wait for the others?"

"There are others coming?" I asked, surprised. "The code on the flyer said you wanted me to come alone."

"We did want you to come alone," she said. "If all of you were together, your trackers would have set off an alarm."

"What do you mean?"

"The radio frequency ID tags they put on you and the rest of your team," she said. "They're not only designed so that Marek's men can find you but also to let them know if you are working together. If any three of the trackers are in the same location other than at school, it sets off an alarm."

"That's why we sent each of you a separate message to lead you to different starting points across the city," said Milton. "It took a lot of planning, but it was necessary, because we can't let Marek find out about this lab. We still have too much work to do."

I looked up at him and suddenly felt panicked.

"Does that mean you invited Natalie? Here?"

Mom gave me a confused look. "Of course we did. We

invited your whole team so we can give you all your new assignment."

This was bad news. If I was right and Natalie was a Level 2, then her learning the location of Mom and Milton's hideout would be a disaster.

"I don't know if that's a good idea," I said.

"Why not?" asked Mom.

Before I could explain, the door opened and Natalie entered with Liberty, who had been her guide like Dr. Stimola was mine. They, of course, had no idea I was just questioning her invitation, so they were all friendly smiles when they came through the door.

"Okay," Natalie said, marveling at the lab. "This may be the coolest place on earth."

"Thank you," said Milton. "I'm pretty fond of it myself."

All of my worlds were colliding, and I was desperately trying to keep calm about it. Somehow I had to tell Mom about my suspicions. She'd know what to do. I turned to talk to her, but Liberty intercepted me and gave me a big hug.

"Hey, Molly, happy belated birthday."

"Thanks," I said.

"Thirteen, right?" he said.

"Let's just hope it's not unlucky thirteen."

I tried to break free from the little conversation, but before I could, Natalie had come over to my mother.

"Where are we exactly?" she asked her. "I tried to keep track of where Liberty was leading me, but I got it all turned around in my head."

Natalie didn't know our exact location and that was good. I didn't give Mom a chance to tell her. Instead, I interrupted and changed the subject.

"What was your clue?" I asked Natalie. "I'm supposedly at a lecture on the birds of Central Park at CCNY."

The sudden change of subject caught her off guard, but one of the advantages of being socially awkward (which I am times a thousand) is that people are used to odd transitions. Rather than wait for an answer to her question, she answered mine.

"I'm at a lecture too," she replied. "It's at the Museum of Natural History, where I'm listening to excruciatingly in-depth analysis of STS-135, the final mission of the space shuttle."

I gave her a confused look. "That was a clue?"

"Since it was the shuttle's last flight, the mission logo was an Omega symbol," she explained.

"And you knew that?"

She smiled sheepishly. "Doesn't everyone?"

Like I said, my worlds were colliding. Here she was, my best friend, a total genius, and I was trying to figure out whether or not she was the enemy.

"So why are we here?" Natalie asked with anticipation. "Are we getting a new assignment?"

"Yes," my mom said. "We want you to—"

"Wait," I said, interrupting again. "We should wait for Grayson and Alex to get here before we talk about anything. That way we'll make sure we all have the same information and there won't be any confusion. And while we're waiting, Mom, I thought you and I might talk for a second . . . alone."

As I moved toward Mom, Natalie looked over at the collection of test tubes and beakers where Milton and my mother had been working.

"What kind of experiments are you working on?" she asked him.

I started to interrupt again, but I didn't really have anything to say. Natalie was frustrated. She started to ask, "Is there a reason you don't want me to . . ." and then she stopped midsentence as she figured it out. The whole room got quiet, and she looked me right in the eyes.

"You know, don't you?" she asked.

"Know what?" I said, trying to play dumb.

"You know exactly what I mean," she said.

I nodded. "Yes," I said softly, "I know."

"When did you figure it out?"

"The day after my birthday, when I came to visit you," I said.

"But you didn't ask me about it."

I shrugged. "I tried to, but I couldn't do it. I kept hoping you would tell me."

She was quiet for a moment, thinking back to that day.

"I almost did," she said. "But I was worried about how you'd take it. I don't mean you specifically, but the three of you. I was especially worried about Alex."

I hate to say it, but I was worried about Alex too. More than any of us, he's distrustful of the undead. It took him way longer to warm up to Liberty than it did the rest of us, and I wasn't sure how he'd respond to finding out about Natalie.

"I would have kept your secret," I said. "In fact, I did keep it. I haven't told anyone. Not even Mom."

"It wasn't a secret to her."

I looked over at my mother.

"The three of us have known since New Year's," she said, nodding toward Milton and Liberty. "We've been working with her and trying to help her adjust to her new life. It's hard, but she's been doing great. I'm really proud of her."

I had only seen my mother once since New Year's and Natalie had seen her multiple times. I'd be lying if I said it didn't hurt my feelings. I understand that Natalie was in an incredibly difficult situation and needed help, but I needed help too. I wanted her to be proud of me, too.

"We thought she should be the one to decide when it was the right time to tell you guys," said Liberty. "I know first hand how difficult that can be."

"That makes sense," I said.

"But I don't understand why you don't want them to tell me where we are or what they're working on, just because I'm undead," she said. "Everyone in this room is, except for you. It shouldn't be a problem."

I didn't know what to say, so I just kept quiet and looked right at her.

"Unless you think I'm a Level 2."

I didn't say yes, but I didn't say no either. I just kept looking at her and watched her face fill with sadness.

"That's it, isn't it?" she asked. "You think I'm an L2."

All eyes were on me, but too much was at stake to do anything but tell the truth.

"Yes, I do."

RUNY

It was terrible. I had just completely devastated my best friend, and I did it right in front of the people who mattered the most to us both. I'd accused her of being a Level 2 zombie. Which is another way of saying I'd accused her of being the enemy. She didn't respond. She just looked like she was about to cry.

"Why would you think that?" asked Mom.

First I hadn't liked the fact that Mom and Natalie had been working together. Now I didn't like that it seemed like she was taking Natalie's side.

"Somebody told Marek about our secret code," I said

pointedly. "Somebody told him that we left messages for each other on the Delacorte Clock. It wasn't me and it wasn't you. Natalie was the only other person who knew."

"You think I told Marek?" Natalie asked, even more shocked than before. "You do realize he's the reason I'm in the condition I'm in? And that I've spent the last three years fighting him?"

"I'm confused," said Milton. "What's this about a code and a clock?"

"The clock by the Central Park Zoo," I told him. "It's where Mom and I agreed to leave messages for each other. Last Christmas Eve, I left one telling her to come to the ice skating rink at Rockefeller Center. Natalie discovered it and surprised us there. That's when she first found out that Mom was undead."

I turned back to Natalie.

"And that's the only time we ever used the clock," I said. "The next time, it was actually Marek using it to lure us. You remember, he did it the same day you told me you were certain that Mom would leave me a message sometime soon. The day you told me to go check it."

"So now you think I'm helping him set a trap for you?" she asked. "After all that we've been through. Don't you remember that I'm the one who asked you to join Omega in the first place? That I'm the one who oversaw your training?"

"I remember all of it, including the part where you said that I should always be careful and assume that anyone who's undead is a Level 2 until they prove otherwise. That it's better to hurt the feelings of a zombie than it is to endanger the lives of your team."

"I would think you'd make an exception for your best friend. After all, I'm not just a zombie. I'm also part of that team you're protecting."

I didn't know how to reply, so things were quiet for a moment. It sounds weird, but the thing that caught my attention was that she considered herself my best friend. Hearing that out loud made my feel even worse about it all.

"By the way, I wasn't the only one who showed up at the skating rink that night," she said. "There was also the zombie who attacked you on the ice. The one who your mother and I had to get rid of. The one who I killed to protect you."

It had never occurred to me that the zombie had seen the message too. I had assumed she just saw me there at the rink and attacked. But it made total sense that she might have uncovered the code just like Natalie had. My mind was racing in reverse.

"Ahh, now you remember," she said, reading my reaction.

"She must have passed the word along to Marek, because I certainly didn't."

It was like a punch to gut. I was suddenly short of breath as I thought through her explanation.

"I'm so sorry," I said. "I forgot all about her."

Natalie went to say something, but my mother interrupted.

"Grayson and Alex are about to get here," she said, pointing at a pair of security monitors that showed them both approaching the lab. "Is this a discussion you want to continue in front of them?"

Natalie looked at me for a moment, then shook her head. "No. It's not."

"Okay," she said. "Molly, knowing what you know now, do you have anything you want to say to Natalie?"

"I really am sorry," I told Natalie. "I was just trying to be careful, and I ended up being stupid."

She seemed unsatisfied with my apology, but with the boys almost to the door she didn't have many options.

"Fine," she said curtly. "Forget about it."

"Good," said my mother. "Because we've got a lot of information to go over."

Moments later Grayson and Alex arrived, and I tried to act like things were normal between us all. Mom and

Milton showed us around the lab, and as they did I noticed Natalie kept her distance from me. Every now and then I caught her glaring my way. I couldn't blame her. I just hoped that the excitement of a new assignment would help distract her from it and make her focus on the work we had to do.

My mother gathered us all around a large wooden table in the corner of the lab and laid out a map of Manhattan.

"Let's talk about RUNY, that's R-U-N-Y," she said. "It stands for Reinventing Underground New York, and it's Marek's big idea. Through his connections with the mayor's office he has taken control of five abandoned subway stations."

She marked them on the map. Three were near each other in Lower Manhattan, another was in Midtown, and the last was on the Upper West Side.

"He is converting them into public areas with restaurants and stores and turning them into underground parks," she continued. "This one even has a playground."

She showed us an architect's rendering of one of the projects. It reminded me of the High Line, which is in the Lower West Side and is about a mile long. Once, it was an abandoned elevated train track, but now it's a public park thirty feet above the ground. Marek was using the same concept, except he was building below the street instead of above.

"It's like he's taking everything about a flatline party and making it permanent," said Alex.

"That's exactly what it is," she replied.

The undead have to go underground for about an hour a day in order to recharge their energy from the Manhattan schist. They often do this at flatline parties, which are held in abandoned sewers and tunnels.

Grayson looked at the drawing and then at all of us. "I know it's Marek and he's evil and all, but this actually sounds like something good. The flatline parties can be scary and dangerous, and this will be much better for everyone. Right?"

"Yes," said Milton. "It's pure genius. He's taking abandoned property that no one else wants and turning it into something useful. And, if all he's doing is making them safe places for the undead, then we're not going to get in his way. But knowing Marek we have to consider that it may be part of something bigger and more sinister. And if that's the case, we have to be prepared to react."

"So what's our assignment?" asked Natalie.

"You're going to find out if RUNY is what he says it is, or if it is what we worry it might be," said Mom.

"Actually," I said, "someone sent me an anonymous letter about this very thing."

Everyone looked at me.

"Who?" asked Grayson.

I gave him a look. "I have no idea. That's why I said it was anonymous."

"And you kept this a *secret*?" Natalie asked. "What's the matter? Didn't you trust us?"

"We weren't supposed to do anything Omega related, so I just kept the letters in my dresser drawer."

"Letters?" she replied. "I thought you said there was *an* anonymous letter. As in one. Now there are letters, plural."

Despite her accusatory tone, I tried to keep my emotions balanced.

"I received two letters," I said. "But only one was about RUNY."

"What did it say?" asked my mother, cutting off our little back and forth drama.

"There was a newspaper clipping about Marek and the ghost stations," I replied. "And a single question written on a piece of paper. 'How is he paying for this?'"

Mom and Milton looked at each other and nodded. "I don't know who sent it," said Mom, "but that's the two-hundred-million-dollar question, because we know he's spent at least that much money so far."

We were all stunned by this number.

"Two hundred million dollars," I said, shaking my head. "Where could he possibly get that much money?"

"That's the key to everything," said Milton. "If we can figure out how he's coming up with the money, then we'll have a better understanding of what he's up to."

"In addition to converting the ghost stations, he's also been doing some other unusual things that appear to be completely random and unrelated," said Mom. "But with Marek, nothing is really ever random. It just looks that way until later on when you see the big picture."

"What types of things?" asked Natalie.

"Out of the blue he donated a lot of money to support the research of one of my colleagues at CCNY," said Professor Stimola. "She's a historian who specializes in the American Revolution."

I instantly thought of the man who attacked my mother and me. I turned to Mom and said, "The guy in the boathouse. He was reading a book about the Revolutionary War."

"It gets better," she replied as she picked up the book off of a nearby table and handed it to me. "This is the book he was carrying."

"*Defending Manhattan: New York City During the Revolutionary War*, by Denise Hendricks," I said, reading from the cover.

"Denise Hendricks is the professor who Marek is suddenly funding," said the professor.

"That does seem like a big coincidence," said Grayson.

"Does she have any particular expertise about George Washington?" I asked.

The professor nodded. "She does. In fact she's writing a biography of him right now. Why do you ask?"

"That was the second anonymous letter," I explained. "It had a map of Manhattan locations that related to Washington, and a note that told me to 'Reserve a place in history.'"

"Any other letters or secrets we should know about?" asked Natalie.

I shook my head. "No. That's it."

I couldn't tell if Grayson and Alex noticed the tension between Natalie and me, but they were probably too excited about the new mission to pay any attention to it.

"What else has been going on with Marek?" asked Grayson.

"There's a company we want to find out about," said Milton. "The Empire State Tungsten Company."

"Back to the man in the boathouse," I said to Mom. "According to his business card he was their vice president."

"That's right," she said. "The company has come up a few

more times in relation to Marek and the Unlucky 13. For example, they just sponsored a fundraiser for the NYPD's brand-new Departmental Emergency Action Deployment Squadron."

"The Dead Squad," said Alex.

"Another amazing coincidence," she replied. "We think these things are all related. We just haven't been able to figure out how, and recent developments have made it almost impossible for us to go above ground to look for answers."

I was trying to figure out what "recent developments" meant when Milton explained.

"She's referring to my brother's current medical state," he said.

We all exchanged confused looks.

"How do you mean?" asked Alex.

"Marek's doctors were able to rebuild him using body parts from my cousins and from my brother Cornelius," he said. "It's quite remarkable, actually. But apparently his body is beginning to reject those parts that came from cousins, while those that came from Cornelius are working perfectly. It seems as though he needs a closer genetic match to make the repairs permanent."

Grayson was the first one of us to really understand what he was implying.

"Do you mean he wants your body parts?" he asked.

"That is *exactly* what I mean," replied Milton.

"As a result, Milton has to keep an extra-low profile," Mom added. "The Dead Squad is looking everywhere for him. They're also on the lookout for me, because they think I'm the way to reach him. That's why we need your help. You can cover more ground than us. You can solve this."

"I've got a plan," said Natalie. "We can only be together as a group at school or else the trackers will go off, right?"

"That's right," said Mom.

"Okay, each one of us will take a specific area," Natalie said, turning to the Alex, Grayson, and me. "Then we'll rotate working in pairs and help each other out. That way we'll follow all the possible leads but also be more likely to see how they come together."

Alex looked to Milton and Mom. "Now you see why we made her the captain."

Mom laughed. "Good choice."

Natalie smiled but otherwise ignored the compliment. She was doing what she did best.

"Grayson, you're going to find out everything there is to know about the Empire State Tungsten Company. Get Zeus on it and start hacking away at every computer database you can find that may be able to help."

"Got it," he said.

"Alex, you know more about the NYPD than all the rest of us combined. Try to figure out as much as you can about the Dead Squad, how they work, and how they're trying to find Milton and Molly's mom."

"My uncle Paul should be able to help with that," he said.

Too much was riding on this, so I decided I had to speak up. "Actually," I said guiltily, "there is something else that I forgot to mention that might be a big help with that."

Everyone looked at me, curious as to what it could be.

"What is it?" asked Natalie. "Another anonymous letter? I thought there were only two."

"No," I responded, more than a little wounded. "I have one of their walkie-talkies. It's set specifically on the band the Dead Squad uses to communicate."

"Seriously?" said Alex. "How did you get it?"

His was not the only expectant look.

"Officer Pell, the one-eared cop who threatened us. Well, the other day he attacked me in Central Park."

That was all I had to say for my mom to respond. "Molly, what did I tell you about—"

"I wasn't doing anything Omega related," I said. "He

just saw an opportunity and he attacked me. I had my back-pack with me; he must have been tracking me at the time."

"Where were you exactly?" asked Mom.

I took a deep breath. "The Blockhouse up in the north-west corner of the park. It was quiet and secluded and we were all alone."

Now the most intense look came from Natalie. The Blockhouse didn't mean anything to the others the way it did to her.

"What were you doing at the Blockhouse?" she asked.

"I was just out exploring. I read about it in a book and wanted to check it out firsthand."

Judging by her expression she didn't necessarily believe this explanation, but the others had no reason to suspect anything so I just kept going.

"Anyway, he attacked me and I beat him back. I don't think I killed him, but I may have. I used the walkie-talkie as a weapon and took it without even realizing I had it with me."

"And what did you do with it after that?" asked my mother. "Have you been eavesdropping on them?"

"No. I turned it off and stuck it in my closet," I said. "I haven't touched it since then. I only kept it because I thought it might be useful in case something like this came along."

"That was good thinking," said Alex. "I'll come by and pick it up later today. If I can listen in on their communication, I can really find out a lot about them. That's huge, Molly."

"Great," I said. I turned back to Natalie and asked, "What's my assignment? Are you and I going to split up the ghost stations?"

"No, I'll take all of those," she said. "I want you to figure out how the Revolutionary War and a history professor fit in to all of this."

I'm going to be honest. My assignment sounded completely boring. I couldn't help but think that Natalie had given it to me as some sort of punishment. But I didn't complain.

We talked for a little bit more about our assignments, and then Grayson asked Milton the same question that Natalie had asked earlier.

"What experiments are you working on?"

He thought about it for a moment before answering. "In a way it's the same experiment I've been working on for the past hundred years. I'm still trying to identify what it is about Manhattan schist that makes all of this possible. How the minerals within a rock keep the undead from dying."

Soon it was time for us to go back. Just as when we'd

arrived, we left with our guides one at a time. Natalie made sure she was the first to leave. My guess is that she didn't want to continue our conversation, and I can't say that I was disappointed. Even though I knew it was unlikely, part of me was hoping that the problem would just go away.

I was the last to leave, which gave me a few minutes to talk to Mom.

"I was just trying to be cautious," I told her once we were all alone.

"I know, sweetie," she replied. "You just have to understand how it sounded to her. She's scared. Her whole world is turned upside down, and now her best friend says that she can't be trusted. It's hard."

I nodded. "I know."

There wasn't really anything else to say about it, so she switched topics. "How's the family?" she asked. "What's going on at home?"

"They're great," I said. "Beth just got a job working in a drama camp this summer. And Dad is, well, he's Dad. He makes it all work out. He told us this great story about when you two were dating and went to the opera."

Mom laughed. "When he confused *La Traviata* and *Il Trovatore*?"

"That's the one."

"That was the night that I knew I loved him," she said.

That comment made me smile. "That's funny, because he said it was the night he knew he loved you, too."

Neither of us said anything for a moment, and then I said, "They miss you so much. I wish they could see you. Like I've gotten to."

She thought about this before replying. "I just don't see how that's possible. I don't see how we can bring them into this world and upend their lives that way. I feel bad enough that it's happened to you."

"I don't feel bad about it at all," I said. "I feel lucky that we have this to share."

Dr. Stimola told me that it was time for us to go, so I said good-bye, and a few minutes later he was leading me back through the catacombs, up the spiral staircase, and into his office. All I could think about was Natalie. Even though I already suspected that she was undead, having it confirmed was intense. I felt terrible for her.

When the professor and I entered the lecture hall, I heard the end of his prerecorded talk.

"Which brings us to the red-tailed hawk," said the voice. "This particular one is named Pale Male. When he was young, he tried to build a nest in a tree in the park but was driven away by a murder of crows. That's right, a group of crows is called a murder. But Pale Male adapted and found a new home on the ledge of a building on Fifth Avenue. He was the first hawk to nest on a building, and with this adaptation he began a dynasty of hawks in Central Park. Today they soar above the park, and like all birds of prey, look for their victims below."

I had heard the story of Pale Male before when I was with the Junior Birders, but this time it made me think of the undead. Just like the hawks, they were driven away from the good parts of the city and forced to adapt. Pale Male chose the ledge of a building, and they picked the underground. And now they had become like birds of prey, keeping their distance and watching potential victims, waiting for just the right moment to strike. I was reminded of this when the lecture ended and I left the building. As I stepped out onto St. Nicholas Terrace, I saw him standing across the street, watching.

He was a cop, a member of the Dead Squad, and it was obvious that he'd been waiting for me. Checking to make sure I was where my transmitter said I was. Circling above, like a red-tailed hawk looking for prey.

Teamwork

The next six weeks reminded me a lot of the training I went through when I first joined Omega. Just like then, I was paired with different teammates on different days. Only now, instead of them teaching me how to break codes and fight zombies, we worked together trying to unravel the mysteries of RUNY. (The other big difference was that now there was an unmistakable sense of tension I had to work through with Natalie as I tried to regain her trust.)

Alex was a total rock star as he figured out the inner workings of the Dead Squad. He used the walkie-talkie I took from Officer Pell and rigged it so that he could hide it in his backpack and listen in on all their communications with a pair of earbuds. He sat in the park every day, and to anyone who happened to notice him, he just looked like a regular teenager listening to music.

"Sometimes I even hear them talking about watching me, while they're watching me," he told me. "It's surreal."

After a couple weeks he was able to determine that there were a dozen officers on the squad and that they had two basic jobs. They were either on Omega detail, which meant they followed us around and searched for Milton and Mom, or they were on protection duty guarding Marek.

Alex's favorite place to eavesdrop on them was at Belvedere Castle in the middle of Central Park. It was designed to look like a castle but is actually home to a nature center and the weather service. Alex liked it because the reception on the top floor observation deck was crystal clear.

"It's so good because the Dead Squad is headquartered in the Central Park precinct of the NYPD," he explained one day when I was with him.

"I wonder why they chose Central Park as their home base?" I asked.

"It took a little research to figure out," he told me.

"But it turns out the Central Park precinct house is made entirely out of Manhattan schist. That way they can be on duty and recharge at the same time."

It was the perfect place for a squad of zombies to work.

Sometimes I joined Alex up on the observation deck and the two of us would plug in and listen together. Usually I could only understand about half of what was being said, because they used a mix of regular English, police terminology, and code words. Like this exchange we overheard:

"Advise, what is Coyote's 10-20?"

"CPW and 70."

It didn't make any sense to me, but Alex leaned over and whispered, "Natalie must be walking home."

"Why do you say that?"

"Coyote's 10-20, that mean's Coyote's location," he said. "Natalie is Coyote, and CPW and 70 is Central Park West and West Seventieth. My guess is she's walking home."

"Natalie is *Coyote*?" I said. "We have code names?"

At first he smiled, but then he cringed and muttered, "Well, yeah."

"What's my code name?" I asked.

"It's not important," he said. "The names don't have

any real meaning. They're just randomly assigned words. Nothing special."

"What is it?" I demanded.

He hesitated before finally giving in. "Gopher."

"*Gopher?* Are you serious?" It took everything I had not to scream at the top of my lungs. "Why am I Gopher?"

"Gophers are really good at digging and tunneling," he said. "You're really good at going underground and finding your way through tunnels. I think it's meant as a compliment."

"A compliment? A gopher is a *rodent*. With huge teeth!" Instinctively I reached up and felt my two front teeth. "Are my teeth oversized?"

"Of course not," he said. "They're perfectly-sized."

"Natalie's Coyote, which is majestic, and I'm Gopher, which is . . . the opposite of majestic. I think I want to file a complaint. What's your code name?"

"You don't want to know," he said.

"Oh, I *want* to know."

He tried not to smile as he said it. "Wolverine."

"Totally unfair. That is the coolest code name in the world."

"Isn't it? I think because I'm such a good fighter." He let out a little growl and did what I can only suspect is a wolverine fighting motion with his hands. (Or should I say paws?)

I know it's ridiculous, but I was offended. I would have kept going on about it, but another transmission caught our attention.

"Advise, what is Eagle's 10-20?"

"Who's Eagle?" I asked. "So help me if that's Grayson's code name . . ."

"No, Eagle is Marek."

Over the radio we heard the response, *"He's home at M42."*

Alex and I both turned and looked at each other at the same time.

"Did he say *home* and *M42*?" I asked.

"He sure did."

This was huge. M42 is a secret bunker located deep below Grand Central Terminal. It was once a CIA safe house but had been taken over by the Unlucky 13. It's where Marek's doctors rebuilt him, and if we heard right, it was also now where Marek lived.

"It makes sense, considering his health," Alex said. "They have everything set up there for treatments and transplants. His doctors can monitor him."

Not once since Omega began in the early 1900s had

we been able to identify an actual home for Marek. It had always been a mystery. But now we thought we had, and after a week of follow up Alex was able to confirm that we were right.

While Alex was having great success with his research into the Dead Squad, Grayson was having a more difficult time learning about the Empire State Tungsten Company. Unfortunately, there was no walkie-talkie-like piece of equipment to help him. He did have Zeus, the most amazing computer I've ever seen, but so far every time he thought he might be on the verge of a breakthrough, he ran into a dead end.

Before I could be any help to him, he had to give me a crash course on the importance of tungsten. He explained that it's a hard metal used in lightbulbs and X-ray machines.

"Does Marek have anything to do with either lightbulbs or X-rays?" I asked.

"Not that I can find," he replied. "But the truth is, I can't find out much about the company, either. They seem to buy a lot of tungsten, but there isn't any record of what they do with it once they get it."

Grayson is out of control smart and great at solving puzzles, and I don't think I had ever seen him so frustrated. Once, he told me he'd spent an entire week working on it without figuring out a single new piece of information. Then one day he asked me to meet him at Leonardo's, a pizza place in Midtown. We ordered a couple slices and ate them as we walked up Lexington Avenue.

"Very good," he said after his first bite. "Sweet and tangy sauce, good firm crust."

Grayson considers himself a pizza expert and is in constant search of the perfect slice. After he took a few more bites, he jotted down some ratings in a little notebook he always carries. Later these would be entered into his pizza database for further referencing. He's designing an app called Perfect Pizza π, but says it's still too early in the development stage for him to share any details with the rest of us.

"Is that why we came here?" I asked. "So you could try out a new slice?"

"No, the slice is my reward for finally making a breakthrough. We're here because of this . . ."

We'd reached the corner of Forty-second and Lex, and he pointed up at the Chrysler Building, which was across the street from where we were standing.

". . . and this."

He pointed to Grand Central Terminal, which was a block away.

"You and Alex discovered that our good friend Marek Blackwell lives deep below Grand Central."

"Right."

"And I was able to identify the headquarters of the elusive Empire State Tungsten Company right there on the fifth floor of the Chrysler Building."

"Interesting," I said. "So you can put Marek within a block of the company."

Grayson smiled. "I can do better than that. After searching through the endless records of companies that own other companies that own other companies, I have finally discovered who actually owns the Empire State Tungsten Company."

"Who is it?" I asked eagerly.

"Ulysses Clark."

Bombshell.

"As in the alias of Ulysses Blackwell? Marek's cousin and financier?"

"The one and only."

We'd always suspected that Ulysses was Marek's second in charge. Not only that, he was also the one who infected the chief of police at last year's Thanksgiving Day Parade. That particular connection might explain why his company was raising money for the chief's Dead Squad.

"So we know for sure that they're connected," I said. "If Ulysses owns the company, that means Marek really owns it. But why is he buying up tungsten? Is he using it as part of his construction at the ghost stations?"

Grayson shrugged. "That's what I'll be trying to figure out as soon as I finish this slice of pizza. I said that I'd made a *little* headway. I still have a long way to go before I can solve it."

It was great to be back in action, but the situation with Natalie was massively frustrating. My hope that the problem would just kind of take care of itself turned out to be wishful thinking. That was obvious the second week when I met her on the sidewalk in front of her apartment building. According to the schedule I was supposed to help her scope out the RUNY construction site at the Worth Street ghost station, but she told me that she was going without me.

"What do you mean?" I asked. "I thought we were going to check it out together."

"I know," she said, "but I just think this would be better considering . . . my situation."

"What situation?"

"The fact that I'm undead," she said. "You remember that, don't you?"

(See what I mean about frustrating?)

"I said I was sorry and I'll tell you I'm sorry as many times as you want," I answered. "I know I was wrong, but I want to make up for it. I was just trying to be careful."

"And that's all I'm doing right now," she replied. "I'm trying to be careful."

"How is going into Dead City by yourself being careful?" I asked.

"I'm not going by myself," she said. "I'm just going *without you*. I have to go underground and recharge anyway, and there's a spot close to Worth Street where I can blend in with the other zombies. I can't do that if you're with me."

As much as it hurt my feelings, this actually made sense. She could dig around much better without me in the way.

"Will Liberty be there?" I asked. "You should have someone from Omega nearby."

"Why? Because Omegas are so trustworthy and reliable? Because an Omega would not hurt me or let me get hurt?"

That was my breaking point, so I just stormed off. Natalie must have realized that she'd pushed too hard, because she ran up and put a hand on my shoulder to stop me. She didn't apologize, but she did soften her tone.

"Liberty will be there," she said.

"Good," I answered. "Be safe."

This pattern of her investigating the construction sites without me continued over the next few weeks. We only worked together as a pair when she was helping me explore Revolutionary War locations. She may have been upset with me, but she still put Omega first and she knew that I needed help.

I was struggling because although there were plenty of places in the city that played a role in the Revolution, I couldn't see what any of them had anything remotely to do with Marek or RUNY.

That's what the two of us were trying to figure out one day up in Washington Heights. At one point during the war the British thought they'd cornered the Continental Army in Brooklyn, but General Washington led a daring escape across the East and Hudson Rivers. If it hadn't been successful, the British might have won the war right then and there. We were trying to follow the route they took across Manhattan to see if it might somehow be useful to Marek today.

We were standing in front of a church, checking a map, when I noticed that Natalie kept clenching her jaw and straining the muscles in her neck.

"Is something wrong?" I asked her.

"Why do you ask?"

"Because you're doing that thing with your neck and jaw."

She gave me a confused look. "What thing."

"Clenching and straining."

She obviously had no idea what I was talking about.

"It's just your imagination," she said.

"No it's not," I said. "You just did it again."

She still had no idea what I was talking and was about to say something snarky, when she made a sudden convulsion and started to cough. She tried to talk again but then there was another convulsion. Finally, she looked right at me with a pained, almost helpless expression and managed to get a sentence out.

"What's happening to me?"

That's when the black liquid started to trickle out of the corner of her mouth.

Help Needed

I was in total panic mode. Natalie had just convulsed twice and a small trail of black liquid had started to come out of the corner of her mouth. The first thing I thought of was the man my mother killed in the boathouse. Black liquid came out of his mouth right before he died.

"Have you been underground to recharge today?"

She tried to talk but she couldn't. Instead she just shook her head.

"What about yesterday?" I asked.

She shook her head again.

"We need to get you recharged right now," I said urgently

as I tried to think of where we could go. I remembered how the Blockhouse worked as a supercharger. It would be perfect, but we were at the corner of Fort Washington Avenue and West 181st Street, and that was at least five miles away.

"Let's get you to the subway station," I said, pointing toward a metro sign just up the street.

She had another convulsion as we walked. I put my arm around her and steadied her by holding her shoulder with one hand and her arm with the other.

"You can make it," I said, trying to convince myself as much as I was trying to convince her. "You are the toughest, strongest person I know, and you can make it."

She was getting weaker, and for the last few steps she staggered and almost fell. Just as we got to the entrance, I realized where we were.

"I've got a better idea," I said. "You just have to make it one more block to Bennett Park."

She gave me a desperate look and managed to force out a single word.

"Under . . . ground."

I thought about the subway station and how hard it would be to get down the stairs to a good location. I was certain I had a better plan.

"This will be better," I said looking deep into her eyes. "Trust me."

She coughed again, and I worried that she might not be able to make it any farther, but she nodded.

"I . . . trust . . . you."

It didn't help that Bennett Park has the highest elevation in all of Manhattan. We had to work our way uphill every step, and over the last fifty yards I was practically carrying her. Luckily, my father had taught me the fireman's carry he learned as a paramedic. I didn't quite have her all the way up on my back, but it was close.

I'm sure she thought I was crazy. But then we made it to the park and my thinking became obvious. The reason Bennett Park is the highest point on the island is because the entire park is built on an outcropping of Manhattan schist that was forced upward during the Ice Age.

We staggered into the park and I gently helped her lie down on the rock formation. An old man was walking his dog and looked over at us to see if we needed any help.

"She's just feeling sick and needs to rest," I said.

He gave us a suspicious look, but his dog was pulling him in a different direction, so he left the two of us alone. I held her head in my lap and talked to her as calmly as I could.

"You're going to be fine," I told her. "We'll stay here for as long as you need."

Her skin was pale, but her eyes looked sharp and I considered that a huge plus. She kept eye contact and I smiled at her.

"I know you're still mad at me and I understand that," I said. "If it helps, you should know that I'm pretty mad at myself too."

She closed her eyes for a moment and I panicked, but when she opened them back up she smiled. "It helps a little," she said in a faint voice.

"Don't talk," I told her. "Just rest."

After about twenty minutes she was strong enough to sit up and talk, and after an hour she regained almost all of her strength.

"You can't do that," I said. "You can't go a whole day without going underground. That's not an option."

"I know," she said. "Although, when I wanted to go underground, you took me here to the highest spot on the island."

We both laughed.

"Well, as you've pointed out, I stick out like a sore thumb down there and I knew this rock would help out."

"You and the parks," she said with a chuckle. "You know them so well."

"Well, this isn't just any park," I told her. "This was the site of Fort Washington, where the father of our country tried to save New York."

"Just like you saved me," she said. "You're my George Washington."

I laughed. It's amazing how much that lifted the guilt I had been carrying around.

"Considering how many times you've saved my life, I figured it was the least I could do."

She reached over and squeezed my hand. "Thank you, Molly."

I still felt guilty about accusing her of being a Level 2, but from that moment on, things were good between Natalie and me.

The next day we were at lunch, telling Alex about Washington's escape across Manhattan (and leaving out the part about Natalie's near death experience), when Grayson showed up excited about something.

"What's up with you?" asked Natalie. "Did some new comic book come out today?"

He gave her a look. "Today is Tuesday. Comic books come out on Wednesdays. If you're going to make sarcastic comments about someone's legitimate interests, you should get your basic facts right."

We all laughed, Natalie loudest of all. "You don't know how much I truly love you, Grayson. You are one of a kind."

"Well, you're about to love me more," he said, "because I think we may have gotten the break we've been looking for."

"What is it?" she asked.

"Empire State Tungsten needs help."

"What do you mean?" asked Alex.

"I found a 'help wanted' listing that they are looking to hire a new data entry person," he said. "That would get us inside the office. That would get us access to data. I'd be able to find out what they're doing with all of the tungsten they're buying."

The three of us exchanged confused looks. "Are you saying that one of us should apply for the job?"

"Yes," he said.

"You get the part that Ulysses Blackwell runs the company," I said. "That's the same Ulysses Blackwell who we fought against in hand to hand combat on New Year's Eve. I'm pretty sure he'd recognize any one of us."

This snag frustrated him.

"I get that," he said. "I'm not saying that we should just walk right in there. But we can put on a disguise and some makeup. We've snuck into flatline parties before. How is this different?"

"For one, it's not a darkened tunnel filled with people trying to get away from a world that despises them," Natalie said.

I hated to think that's how she saw her condition.

"And if you remember, we barely made it out of a couple of those parties as it is. Now you're talking about going into a professional situation at a time when the undead are ready to launch a war against us if they get the slightest hint we're causing problems. When it comes to acting, we're not that good."

He slumped as he realized she was right. He was so close to reaching something that had eluded him for weeks. But it was still out of reach.

Or was it?

"You know who is that good at acting?" Alex asked.

Grayson thought about it for a moment and smiled. "You're absolutely right."

"Who?" asked Natalie.

"Molly's sister," said Alex.

"Beth?" I asked. "Now you guys really have gone nuts."

"Have we?" asked Grayson. "She's super talented. Remember all those voices she did at your party. She'd be amazing."

"And, Ulysses doesn't know her at all. None of the

undead know her. They can't recognize somebody they've never seen before."

Natalie and I exchanged a look. "And the part about her not being an Omega," I said. "What's your solution for that?"

"I don't know," said Grayson. "But Milton said it himself. If we can figure out how Marek's paying for this, then we have a good chance of figuring out why he's doing what he's doing. I've tried everything I can to find out what this company is up to, and I've come up dry. This may be our only real chance."

"You want *my* sister to get a job at Empire State Tungsten?"

"I don't want her to get the job," he said. "I just want her to apply for it. That way she can go in there and get a look around. The smallest piece of information might be all we need."

It seemed utterly impossible, but I also knew that he might be right about one thing. It might be the only way for us to find what we were looking for. So even though the idea was totally bananas, that night I knocked on the door of Beth's room.

"Come in," she said.

She was at her desk, doing homework, when she looked up at me.

"I have a question I want to ask you," I said.

"It must be important if you knocked," she said. "You never knock."

"It is important," I said. "But it's also . . . confusing."

Beth laughed. "Sometimes you really are strange, you know that?"

"You have no idea how strange. Anyway, I want to ask you for a favor, but I can't explain *why* I need the favor. You just have to trust me that it really is important."

I expected her to kick me out right then, but she didn't. Instead she turned in her seat and looked right at me, a curious look on her face.

"Does this have something to do with Omega?"

The Job Interview

I stared at Beth, totally astounded. "You know about Omega?"

She smiled. "I guess I do. At least sort of. About a month before Mom died, I was hanging out with her at the hospital. I forget where you and Dad were, but it was just the two of us. And ice cream. Even though she wasn't supposed to have any, she'd smuggled a quart of Rocky Road into her room and said we had to 'destroy all the evidence before the nurses came back.' So we just sat there with two spoons and ate it right out of the carton while we talked."

"What did you talk about?" I asked.

"Boys . . . college . . . you name it. She wanted to cover as many topics as possible, all the things we wouldn't get the chance to talk about later. She told me some great stories, some embarrassing ones, and gave me advice, a lot of which I'll pass on to you when the time is right. It was the most perfect hour of my life. In a year filled with so many terrible memories, it's the only great one."

"So what does that have to do with Omega?"

"We were laughing about something, and then from out of the blue she said that one day you might come to me asking for a favor that didn't make much sense. Apparently she knew what she was talking about because that's just what you did. And she said that even if it sounded really strange, before I said no I should ask you if it had to do with Omega."

"And if it did?" I asked.

"Then she told me I should do it, no questions asked."

I couldn't believe it. That is so like my mother to foresee this situation, and even more like Beth to go along with it.

"Well she was right," I said. "This favor is for Omega."

"Then I'm in," she replied. "Just tell me what you need."

"That's it? You really aren't going to ask me why?"

"I gave my word, little sister," she said. "If we lose faith and trust, then we've lost everything."

It sounded just like something Mom would say. It's funny. People always think that I'm like her because I love science and because I inherited her mismatched eyes. As far as I'm concerned, it's the biggest compliment in the world. But the truth is, I think that Beth is the one who's more like her. They both have a blend of confidence and compassion that I could never hope to pull off. I walked over and gave her a hug.

"Thank you."

"I told her I'd do it," she said.

"Not about that," I replied. "Thank you for being such a great sister."

She hugged me back, and it took me a moment before I could move on. Finally I let go and we both wiped some tears from our eyes.

"All right," she said. "Tell me what I have to do for this favor."

"You have to do what you do best," I said. "You have to act."

I gave her the basics about the job opening, and the next day after school Grayson came over and filled her in on some specifics. He wanted her to look for anything she could find out about what was happening to the tungsten the company was buying. He also said it would be great if she could get the names of any of the employees.

Beth scheduled an interview for the following day. Unfortunately, the only time they had open was at three thirty. Since we didn't get out of school until three, that didn't leave us much time to get there and be close by if she needed any help.

Alex, Grayson, Natalie, and I practically sprinted the moment the bell rang. We didn't have time to come up with an elaborate plan for our trackers, so we just split into pairs and kept away from each other.

Alex and I took the subway and went to Leonardo's, the pizza place a block from the Chrysler Building. Meanwhile, Grayson and Natalie rode the Roosevelt Island tram across the river and then took a cab to Grand Central. All of us were close by, but hopefully we weren't close enough to each other to set off any alarms with the Dead Squad.

Five minutes before her interview was scheduled Beth and I exchanged texts.

BETH: *Getting on the elevator. Feeling very employable.*
MOLLY: *Good luck! Text the moment you're done.*

And that was it.

As nerve-wracking as it is to go undercover or do any

kind of secret surveillance, it's far worse when you have to sit and wait while someone else does it. Everything is out of your control, and all you can do is worry. What made this especially bad was that it was all new to Beth and she didn't really know what she was getting into.

"Relax," Alex said when he noticed that I was nervously twisting the straw from my soda. "She's going to do fine."

"What are they saying?" I asked, motioning to the walkie-talkie in his backpack.

"Nothing unusual," he said, trying to reassure me. "Everything is okay."

In the course of the next five minutes, I must have checked my watch about forty times. I already regretted putting her in this position.

"Would you like to listen in?" Alex asked, hoping it might calm my nerves if I had something to do.

"Yeah. That would be good," I said.

I moved to the other side of the table and sat next to him in the booth. He only had one pair of earbuds, so we had to sit close together and share, each of us using one from the same set. Their conversations were filled with police lingo, so I didn't understand a whole lot of what was being said, but there was no sense of urgency or alarm. I took that as a good sign.

When I checked my phone again, it was 3:55. I figured she would be done at any moment. Then I heard a call on the radio.

"Advise. Eagle is on the move with full detail."

"Eagle's Marek, right?" I asked, even though I knew the answer. It was just nervous chatter.

"That's right, and full detail refers to all the cops that protect him. He normally only travels with all of them if something big is happening."

The message continued. *"There is a change of schedule. Rather than WSS, he is headed to Test C."*

"What are WSS and Test C?" I asked.

"WSS is Worth Street station, it's one of the RUNY construction sites," he said. "But I don't know what Test C is. I've never heard that one before."

I took another bite of my slice of pizza and checked my phone again. It was now 3:57. I had to calm my nerves. I closed my eyes and took a deep breath. It was an exercise we'd learned in jeet kune do. Real masters could do it and significantly lower their heart rate. It also helps clear your mind, and it must have worked because once I tried it I only needed about twenty seconds to figure out what Test C was code for.

"Beth!" I said as I bolted from the table toward the

door. I'd forgotten that I had the earbud in, and when I started running it popped out of my ear and flew back at Alex, flicking him in the face. I was halfway to the Chrysler Building before he caught up to me on the sidewalk.

"What's going on?" Alex asked as he ran with me stride for stride.

"Test C," I said, picking up speed. "It stands for The Empire State Tungsten Company. Marek just changed his plans to go there. They must have figured out who Beth really is."

Eagle's Nest

I sprinted full speed until we reached the entrance of the Chrysler Building. That's when I decided I should at least try to blend in. After all, it's a workplace and we didn't want to attract any extra attention. I took a deep breath and calmly walked through the revolving door. When I got inside, I was surprised to see Grayson and Natalie in the lobby. They could tell I was upset.

"Marek is heading to the office," I explained.

"We know," Natalie said. "We saw him walk through Grand Central with his police escort. We followed him outside to see where he was going, and when he went into the building we put two and two together."

"We called to tell you," Grayson said. "But you didn't answer."

I must not have heard my phone ring as I ran down the street. I beelined straight for the elevators, and the others were right behind me.

"We'll bust in if we have to. I can't let them hurt my sister," I said. "I should never have asked her to do this. This is all my fault."

We got on an elevator and I jabbed the button for five a few times, rapid fire.

"You've got to calm down, Molly," Alex said. "No matter what is happening, keeping calm is our best approach."

I closed my eyes and waited for the ding to signal that we'd reached the fifth floor. Until then I practiced my jeet kune do breathing exercise so I could focus all my energy and anger. By the time the elevator stopped, I was ready to take on an undead army all by myself if I had to.

The bell rang and I opened my eyes just as the doors opened onto the fifth floor. I was prepared to storm into battle, but then I saw something that made me stop cold. My sister was standing there waiting to take the elevator back down to the lobby.

"What are you doing here?" she asked confused. "I

thought I was supposed to meet you at the pizza place."

My mind spun rapidly, trying to figure out what was going on.

"Beth?"

"Actually, today I am playing the role of Sabrina, aspiring data entry specialist. I think the interview went really well."

I still couldn't make sense of it all.

"But what about Marek? Didn't he come into the office?"

"You mean Mr. Big Shot with the bodyguards," she said. "Oh, he came in all right. Everyone got very excited and rushed into a back room. Some big deal is about to go down. It was perfect, because they just kind of left me there unattended and I was able to get this."

She held up a flash drive.

"What's that?" asked Grayson.

"Only everything you ever wanted to know about the Empire State Tungsten Company, and more."

It's amazing how quickly the mood changed from panic to joy. Beth stepped on the elevator and we were all ready to high-five. She had executed the plan better than we could have hoped, and our anxiety had all been a mistake.

"Seriously," I said catching my breath, "that's amazing. You're amazing."

"Let's get out of here," Natalie said as she reached down to press the button for the lobby.

"Stop!" Alex reached out and grabbed her arm. He was listening in on the walkie-talkie, and something made him grimace. "They know we're here."

"What do you mean?" asked Grayson.

"The four of us are together in one place," he explained. "We set off the alarm."

In our panic, we had all completely forgotten about the trackers.

"Then we better hurry up," said Natalie.

"It's too late. Since Marek's in the building, there are already some Dead Squad members in the lobby," he replied. "We have to go up."

He pressed the button for sixty-one, and the elevator came to life and started climbing.

I looked up at the numbers changing on the display above the doors and felt a new sense of panic. "Are you sure we need to go that high?" I asked.

"I'm sorry, Molly, but you're just going to have to deal with your fear of heights," said Alex. "This is an emergency. They're going to outnumber us, so we need to get high enough to really weaken them."

Actually, it wasn't my fear of heights that had me concerned. I was worried about Natalie. Going that high would weaken her, too. I tried to check her reaction without drawing attention to what I was doing. I could tell she was nervous. Neither of us wanted a repeat of what happened in Washington Heights. The vision of her spitting out black liquid was already haunting me. I figured we could stay up there for about fifteen minutes at the most before the height would begin to affect her. That didn't leave me much time.

"Why the sixty-first floor?" asked Grayson. "That seems kind of random."

"It's not," said Alex. "Whenever we're going into an operation I try to work out escape plans in case something goes wrong. I researched the building last night and discovered that the sixty-first floor used to have an observation deck, but now it's closed and abandoned, which makes it an ideal place for us to hide and wait them out."

"Wait them out?" I asked. "Is that our plan?"

"Unless you've got a better one," he said.

I didn't, but I knew that one wouldn't work because waiting was exactly what Natalie couldn't do. "What do you think?" I asked her. "Do you have a different plan?"

It was the first time I ever saw her at a loss for words. She didn't say anything, which the others probably took as her agreeing to the idea. Instead of Natalie, the next person who talked was my sister.

"I know I told you guys that I'd do the favor no questions asked," she said. "But since the favor part's over, would someone mind telling me what the heck is going on?"

I was a mental mess. I still hadn't recovered from the thought that Marek was going to attack Beth. I was worried about taking Natalie up to a dangerous height. And a team of zombies was about to come and attack. I didn't really have any room in my brain to come up with a good explanation, so I just blurted out the truth.

"Omega is a secret society that protects the city from the undead. Marek is their leader and now they're coming to fight us."

For a moment the only sounds in the elevator were the whirring of the motor and the lame music playing over the speaker. The five of us were silent until the bell dinged and the doors opened.

"You mean zombies?" she said, incredulous.

"Actually, they hate being called the Z word," Alex said as he got off and held the doors for the rest of us. "But that's exactly what she means."

I thought back to when they first told me about Omega. We were at Grayson's house, and I was ready to storm out because I thought they were making fun of me. But Beth's reaction was . . . *different*.

She smiled as she considered it and tried to read our expressions. "You know, I almost believe you guys."

"Well, in a couple minutes I think you're going to be convinced," Alex replied. He unplugged his earbuds from the walkie-talkie and turned it up so that we all could hear.

"Affirmative, Home Base, Eagle is secure. Omega is between the fifty-eighth and sixty-third floors, and we are sending up a team to isolate. We are go to engage Omega."

"We caught a break there," Alex said.

"How is that a break?" asked Grayson. "They're coming up to *isolate* us. That doesn't sound like a break."

"But they don't know the exact floor we're on," he said. "The trackers are designed to show where you are on a map, not how high you are in the air. That should buy us an extra minute or two to get ready."

He led us down the hall and forced open a door to reveal a big room that was in the middle of a remodeling project. It was filled with scaffolding, tools, and giant plastic sheets hanging from the ceiling. There were also picture windows that looked out over a terrace and toward downtown. Even for someone normally terrified of heights, I had to admit that it was an amazing view of the city.

"I read about it last night," Alex said. "They're turning it into a restaurant called the Eagle's Nest."

"Not eagle because of Marek's code name?" I asked.

"No," he said. "Because of them."

He pointed out toward the terrace. At each corner there was a giant silver eagle-gargoyle.

"They're beautiful," Grayson said. "I've always wanted to see them up close."

"Gargoyles are supposed to scare off bad spirits," Alex said. "Let's hope they scare off zombies, too."

In my desperation I came up with a plan to get Natalie downstairs.

"I think we need to get the flash drive to safety," I said. "Let's give it to Natalie and she can take the stairs. That way the information will be protected."

"They've probably stationed someone in each stairwell," Grayson said.

"Maybe," I said. "Even so, Natalie can handle one zombie by herself, and once she does it's all clear sailing."

"That's not a bad idea," Alex said, much to my relief. "But we can't afford to lose Natalie, she's too good a fighter. We should send Beth. No one on the Dead Squad knows who she is."

"You don't know me either," Beth said to Alex. "Not

if you think I'd leave my sister in this situation. If there's going to be a fight, I'm going to be part of it."

"It's not like in the movies," Grayson said. "These are what we call Level 2s. They're aggressive, determined, and . . . really disgusting,"

Beth smiled. "You just described all the boys at my school. I'll be fine."

I loved Beth's attitude, but I had to keep my focus on Natalie and getting her downstairs. "We need to get the flash drive out of here," I said forcefully. "And it has to be Natalie!"

"What is going on with you about this?" Grayson asked. "We need Natalie with us because some very scary creatures are about to come here looking for us."

"They're not creatures!" I snapped. "And they're not zombies! They're people. They're undead, but they're still people."

Natalie smiled. "It's okay. I know what he means."

"We are almost out of time here," Alex said. "So if you two want to explain whatever is going on here, it would be great."

Natalie took a deep breath and turned to the boys.

"I'm undead."

Before they could even respond, the elevators chimed in the hallway. Someone was coming for us.

61 Stories

I watched their faces as they reacted to the news. Grayson looked sad, but Alex seemed angry. This was what Natalie and I had been so worried about. Neither one of us knew how he would take the news.

"Take it back!" he demanded. "You cannot be undead. Take it back."

"I can't," Natalie replied softly. "Because I am."

Alex started taking deep breaths, trying to keep his emotions under control while Grayson went over to her and gave her a hug, just like I expected he would.

"I'm so sorry," Grayson said to her. "I'm so sorry."

Natalie rested her head on his shoulder for a moment, but before there could be any real emotion between the two of them we were interrupted by a transmission over the walkie-talkie.

"I'm getting a reading on the sixty-first floor," said the voice. "I'll check for visual confirmation."

This development snapped us out of the moment. Well, all of us except for Alex. He couldn't have cared less about the Dead Squadder in the hallway. He was too focused on Natalie.

"How is this possible?" he asked. "How did it happen?"

"It was during the fight on New Year's," she said.

"No, that's not what I mean," he said. "I mean, how did it happen to *you*? I've gone through this a thousand times in my head and every time it's the same. It's supposed to be me."

We were all confused by this.

"What's supposed to be you?" asked Natalie.

"It's simple mathematics," he said. "When you consider the number of times we get into these situations, the odds are that one of us would become undead. But that's why I always go first. That's why I always keep a lookout. It's to skew those odds toward me. My job is to protect you. If it's going to happen, it's supposed to happen to me."

"It's not your job to protect me," she said. "It's our job to look out for each other."

He was totally devastated, and I had no idea what he was going to do next.

"The reading on sixty-one is very hot," came an announcement on the walkie-talkie.

"Let us know the moment you have visual confirmation?" came the reply. *"If you do, we will send a team immediately."*

"Alex," said Grayson, pointing at the walkie-talkie. "We're about to have company."

"I'm a little busy dealing with something Grayson," Alex said, perturbed. "I need a second, all right?"

"I don't know if we have a second."

We could hear the zombie in the hallway as he checked doors to see if they were unlocked. He was getting closer.

We all looked at Alex, trying to figure out his next move.

"Fine," he said, totally annoyed. He took a deep breath and marched right out toward the hallway.

"What are you doing?" asked Natalie.

He didn't answer. Instead he just walked out the door, and we heard the following over the walkie-talkie.

"I hear a door opening and . . . wait . . . I have visu—" and then static as the transmission went dead.

Seconds later Alex came back through the door. In

one hand he held a walkie-talkie, and with the other he dragged the body of the dead zombie.

"Here's an extra walkie," he said, tossing it to Grayson. "Beth, this is what a zombie looks like. When they attack, go for the head."

The speed with which he took care of the situation was amazing, but while we were all stunned, Alex just picked up the conversation where he left off as if nothing had happened.

"How could you not tell me?" he asked Natalie.

She looked at him for a moment, trying not to get emotional.

"I know what you think of them . . . ," she said, motioning to the dead zombie on the floor. ". . . I mean, what you think of *us*. . . . I'm one of them now."

"You are not one of *them*," he said, his voice rising. "You're one of *us*! *We* are a team. It doesn't matter if you are living or undead, you will always be one of us. Omega today, Omega forever!"

Natalie blinked a couple times, and when she opened her eyes all the way, a tear streamed down her face. It was black, but it was a tear.

"Does that mean you still want me on your team?" she said, looking Alex in the eye.

He wiped the tear off her cheek with his thumb.

"Always," he said. "No matter what."

She hugged him tightly.

We heard an elevator ding in the hallway and the sounds of a group of people stepping out.

"It's really great that you have this whole 'them and us' thing figured out," Grayson said. "But that noise you hear out there? That really is *them*, and they are coming for us. So we have to get ready."

Alex and Natalie redirected their attention from each other and looked to us. We were out of time and we needed to brainstorm.

"You're the one who came up with this escape plan," I said to Alex. "What do we do?"

"Natalie's situation changes everything," he said. "We've got to get her downstairs fast."

"Easier said than done," I said, looking out toward the hall filled with zombies. "How do we do that?"

"I've got it," said Grayson, excited. "I actually think I've got it. They're looking for four of us. But we've got an extra person. Beth can become Natalie."

I didn't understand what he was getting at, but Alex was right with him.

"That's brilliant," he said. "If Natalie gives Beth her jacket and if Beth pulls her hair back like Natalie's, it just might fool them. At least long enough for what we need."

Natalie was wearing a light denim jacket, which she quickly handed to Beth. Beth slipped it on and pulled her hair back in a ponytail.

"Nat, you hide in here and we'll go out on the terrace," Alex said. "They'll be looking for four people, so when they see us they'll head out there and walk right by you. That should give you plenty of time to escape. Once they realize it's really Beth, you'll be long gone."

"That's not fair to Beth," she said. "I can make it about fifteen minutes before there's a problem. They're in the same situation as I am. Whatever happens is going to be fast and like you said, I'm a good fighter."

"There's no time to debate," he said. "They're here and you're going!"

Sure enough, we could hear them trying to open the door. Reluctantly Natalie ducked behind some of the construction equipment, and the rest of us went out on to the terrace.

"Just act like we're enjoying the view," said Alex.

We lined up along the railing and looked out over the city. I was terrified for so many reasons, I couldn't really worry about the height. Although it was awfully high. We heard a voice crackle over Alex's walkie-talkie.

"We have visual confirmation. All four of them are on the terrace on the sixty-first floor. Repeat: All four of them are on the terrace on the sixty-first floor. Everyone engage."

"Part one worked," Alex said. "They think we're all out here. Are you guys ready for part two?"

"Definitely," I said.

"Me too," said Grayson.

"I'll guess we'll find out," added Beth.

Moments later the doors to the terrace opened and we could hear the Dead Squad come outside behind us. We tried to stay cool and kept looking out over the city.

"Don't turn around until you have to," I whispered to Beth. "I will protect you no matter what."

"What seems to be the problem, officer?" Alex said, turning and engaging the leader of the group.

"You know what the problem is," he said. "Marek was clear that the four of you are not supposed to get together. He told you there'd be war. You have been warned, so what happens next is entirely your fault."

Grayson and I both turned, but Beth kept looking out toward downtown. There were eight of them in total. Three, including the one in charge, were dressed in NYPD uniforms. The others were your typical Level 2 lowlifes. They were big, especially the cops, but I thought we could handle them.

"Actually," I said interrupting. "Marek said we cannot engage in Omega activity . . . and we're not. We're just up here enjoying the view. It really is amazing."

The man evaluated the situation for a moment and then turned his attention toward Beth.

"What about you, Coyote?" he said, using Natalie's code name. "You just enjoying the view."

Beth dragged it out for as long as she could before she turned around. When she did, his face filled with rage.

"Who are you?" he demanded.

"I guess I'm Coyote," she said. Then for fun she made a little howling noise.

He was not amused. He turned to the others and said, "Coyote's not here."

He grabbed his walkie-talkie and started to make a transmission. "Coyote is—"

That's as far as he got. Alex kicked the walkie-talkie out of his hand, and our chance for a peaceful encounter was over.

They outnumbered us, so it was important to strike quickly. I did a full roundhouse kick that took out the zombie nearest me, instantly bringing their number down to seven. Next I double-punched another in the stomach, dropping him to his knees, but before I could deliver the knockout shot, I was blindsided by one of the cops.

He was big and smelled disgusting. He slammed me into the railing so that I hit it with my stomach, which bent me over and gave me a dizzying view of the ground more than 650 feet below me. Pain radiated from my gut, and the angle made me a little dizzy as I tried to fight back. Then he added insult to injury when he put his lips right next to my ear and said, "Ready to see if gophers can fly?"

That did it. I really hate that code name.

I slammed my head directly back into him and snapped my body upright so that it pushed him away. I spun around and delivered a punch right to his chest.

"I want a new code name!" I said as I added a flurry of punches, which he deflected.

He was tough and seemed to relish the challenge as he charged right back at me. He was just about to hit me, when I got help from an unlikely source. Out of nowhere Beth came in and took him out with a devastating flurry of kicks to his shins and forearms before dropping him with a punch right to the middle of his forehead. It was a blistering attack that left me momentarily speechless.

"You know krav maga?" I asked stunned.

"I do, but that was actually muay thai," she said. "It's easy to confuse the two, because they use a lot of the same elements."

I was flabbergasted. Here I thought I had been living with a cheerleader all these years, and it turned out she was a lethal weapon. She enjoyed my sense of astonishment and just smiled and winked at me.

"What?" she said. "You thought that only you and Mom had secrets?"

This was a game changer.

Beth and I had taken out two, and when I looked over at Alex I saw one dead zombie on the floor while he fought another one. The odds were evening out, but there were still five of them, and Grayson was struggling with one. The cop had him wrapped up from behind in a full chest hold and was lifting him up in the air.

"Kick him, Grayson," I yelled.

He tried to kick backward with his heel, but he was at an awkward angle and he couldn't get any power into it.

I moved to help, but I was grabbed from behind and slammed down onto the terrace floor. A tall L2 loomed over me and tried to hold me down by shoving his boot into my stomach, which was still sore from getting folded over the railing. I saw that both Alex and Beth were busy, which meant that none of us could help Grayson.

The zombie had lifted him completely into the air, and despite Grayson's flailing he had no problem carrying him.

In a flash I thought back to Grayson's frustrations that Alex was always the hero and that he was never any good in these fights. I'm sure that frustration was only making the situation worse for him. Then I realized what the zombie was planning to do. He was carrying him over to the edge and was going to throw him off of the building.

"Grayson!" I screamed.

I tried to get up, but the zombie still held me down, his boot digging deep into my stomach. I reached up and twisted his knee until it dislocated, green slime shooting out where the bone punctured the skin. Then I punched the other knee from the side so that he fell. Unfortunately, he landed directly on top of me, which kept me from jumping right up to help.

I could see the panic in Grayson's face as the zombie neared the edge.

"Use the railing!" I yelled to him. "Push back off of the railing."

Grayson did exactly what I said. He pushed back off of the railing and drove his body into the zombie, knocking him back. It was a good move, but the zombie was big and bad and it only slowed him down for a second. I scrambled to get back on my feet, but I was too far away to help. So were Beth and Alex.

"No!" I screamed as they neared the edge.

They say that time slows down in your head at moments of great stress, and I've had that feeling. But this was the opposite, it seemed like everything was moving too fast for me to do anything about it. That's why it was such a surprise when a punch came out of nowhere and connected to the back of the zombie's head.

Natalie.

She had come back to help. She delivered a quick series of blows to his lower back, and the zombie loosened his grip, allowing Grayson to break free. She continued her vicious attack, as did we all. Within less than a minute, all of the zombies lay dead on the floor.

"What are you doing here?" Alex demanded. "I thought I told you to go downstairs and be safe."

"Really? Because I thought you told me that we were always a team no matter what," she replied. "Something like 'Omega today, Omega forever'."

She looked around at all of the dead bodies and smiled.

"Besides, I'm still the captain of this team," she added. "You don't tell me what to do. I tell you what to do."

She laughed, and it was by far the happiest I'd seen her since New Year's. For the first time since that day, we were truly a team again.

"We better get you out quickly," Alex said. "They'll send another team right away."

She shook her head. "I don't think so. At least not for a while."

She grabbed the walkie-talkie and turned up the volume so we could all hear.

"All units, trackers report that all four Omegas have left the building and are now walking north on Lexington."

We all gave Natalie a confused look. "Why do they think we're walking down Lex?"

"While you guys were fighting, I collected all the trackers and slipped them into the pocket of a pizza delivery guy on the elevator."

Alex laughed. "Seriously?"

"Totally," she said. "It should buy us some time."

"Advise all units, I'm on Lexington and do not see them. This must be a mistake. Does anyone have a visual on the Omegas?"

Beth reached down and picked up the walkie-talkie. We had no idea what she was doing, but she pressed the talk button and responded. Only, she didn't sound like Beth Bigelow, she used one of the accents she'd demonstrated for the boys at my birthday party.

"That's affirmative," she said, sounding just like a cop

from Brooklyn. "I have eyes on Coyote right now. She is entering a pizzeria."

"His shirt said Leonardo's," whispered Natalie.

"Roger that," Beth added, now switching over to a Bronx accent. "I see her too. She's entering Leonardo's Pizzeria. Repeat, Leonardo's Pizza."

We all marveled at what she was doing. Alex got her attention and pointed at each one of us as he told her our code names.

"Wolverine, Jayhawk, and Gopher."

She gave me a raised eyebrow look and whispered, "Gopher?"

"It's not like I picked it."

"Coyote is with Wolverine, Jayhawk, and Gopher," she said with yet another accent. "All four of them have entered the pizzeria."

"Roger that. All units advance to Leonardo's Pizzeria at Forty-third and Lexington."

She looked up at us and smiled.

"That should give you a few minutes to get out of the building before they figure out you're not in the pizzeria."

We took the elevator down to the third floor. Then we went down the rest of the way by the stairs on the opposite side of the building. By the time we reached the subway station we were equal parts exhausted, ecstatic, and relieved. Grayson took the flash drive, and Alex insisted on escorting Natalie home.

We all exchanged hugs on the platform, even Beth.

Once everyone had gone, Beth and I just stood there looking at each other. So much of the afternoon had been about surviving the attack and the boys learning about Natalie. I hadn't gotten the chance to check on how Beth was handling all of this.

"Let's head home," she said. "You have some explaining to do."

I thought about it for a second. "I'll explain, but first I need to show you something."

We took the subway north to City College and were quiet for most of the ride.

"When did you learn krav maga and . . . what was it?"

"Muay thai," she said.

"That," I said. "When did you learn martial arts?"

"Mom insisted that I do it when I was a kid, and I always kept with it," she replied. "I kind of kept it hidden because I didn't want to catch any flack from the girls in the building or at school."

That's when it dawned on me that Mom might have trained Beth for Omega just like she trained me.

"Did she make you learn the periodic table, too?" I asked.

"Yeah," she said. "How'd you know that?"

I shook my head, disbelieving.

"She was preparing you in case you became an Omega," I said. "She did the same thing with me. The periodic table is the key to our code."

We got off the subway and started walking to the college.

"If I was trained like you, then why didn't I become an Omega?" she asked. "Am I not good enough?"

"Hardly. You'd be awesome at it," I said. "What you did up there was amazing."

"Then why?" she asked.

"It's because you have to go to MIST."

"Oh," she said, a look of disappointment on her face. "I guess I screwed that up."

"What do you mean?"

"It's what Mom wanted, and I wouldn't do it," she explained. "She asked me to apply, but I told her I didn't want to go there. That must have really disappointed her."

"You can't think that," I said. "You never disappointed Mom. She was always proud of you."

Beth sighed. "I guess we'll never really know for sure."

And this is where I had her. She followed me as we snuck down into the catacombs below CCNY. I couldn't remember all of the turns by heart, but I quickly realized that the pipes would help me find my way. The pipes ran along the ceiling but came down the wall by the secret entrance.

Beth hardly asked any questions, no doubt overwhelmed by everything from the zombie attack to our discussion of Mom. Finally, I found the wall and made sure to remind myself which pipe was the right one.

I turned the wheel and the hidden door unlocked. Just as I went to pull it open, I turned to Beth and said, "If you don't believe me when I say you never disappointed her, you can just ask her yourself."

I opened the door to reveal the hidden lab. Milton and my mother were working on an experiment and looked up, surprised by the interruption. Then Mom saw my sister and took off her safety glasses.

"My dear, sweet Elizabeth," she said, shaking her head.

I looked at my sister as tears streamed down her face.

"Mom?"

George Washington Walked Here

It had been two weeks since our adventure at the Chrysler Building, and the results had been both emotional (Beth and Mom's tearful reunion) and educational (all the information Grayson had retrieved from the files of the Empire State Tungsten Company). But so far they hadn't been dangerous. Marek had yet to deliver on his threat to start an all-out war between the undead and Omega, and that had us worried.

Not that you could tell from the oh-so-enlightening conversation the boys were having as Grayson, Alex, and I looked across the harbor at the Statue of Liberty.

"Did you ever notice that the Statue of Liberty's butt is pointed right at New Jersey?" Grayson asked. "I mean, that's their view."

"Maybe they should put that on the license plates," replied Alex. "New Jersey—the Butt of Liberty."

We were waiting in Battery Park at the southernmost tip of Manhattan. In addition to its view of the harbor, the park is the starting point of the George Washington walking tour of New York City. The tour was laid on the map that my anonymous informant mailed to me. I wanted to walk it as part of my search to see what the father of our country had to do with Marek Blackwell's plan to reinvent underground New York. But, since we didn't know when Marek was going to strike back, the others thought it would be safer if they came along.

"You know, I've never even been there," I said, pointing at the statue. "My whole life in New York and I've never been to the Statue of Liberty."

"Me neither," said Alex.

Grayson shook his head. "Molly I understand, because she's terrified of heights, but why not you?"

"No reason," Alex said. "It's just something you figure you'll get around to one day, so there's no rush. Every time

I thought about going, I put it off because I knew I'd get another chance."

We were all quiet for a moment, and then Grayson said something that revealed what was on all of our minds.

"I wonder if Natalie thought the same thing," he said. "I wonder if she thought she'd do it sometime and never got around to it. 'Cause she sure can't do it now."

The three of us had not really talked about Natalie's situation yet.

"I think about stuff like that all the time," Alex said. "I think about all the things she can't do. All the places she'll never get to go."

"Do her parents know?" asked Grayson.

"They must," said Alex. "After all, they moved from the twelfth to the second floor."

They both turned to me. "How'd they take it?" asked Grayson.

I shrugged. "I don't know," I said. "Natalie and I weren't really talking much in the month and a half after I found out, so I never got the chance to ask her about her parents."

"Why weren't you talking?" asked Alex.

I took a deep breath and closed my eyes, embarrassed by what I was about to say. "I accused her of being a Level 2."

They both laughed.

"That must have been fun," said Grayson.

"Did she try to rearrange your face?" asked Alex.

I thought about it for a moment, then asked them, "Is it really that impossible to believe? I mean, did either of you two think she might be an L2?"

"For about a nanosecond," said Grayson. "But we were about to fight the Dead Squad. It was pretty obvious what side she was on. I might have wondered about it if it had just come up in conversation."

"Not me," said Alex. "But I can understand why you would."

"Why not you?" I asked.

Alex thought about it for a moment. "The best that I can understand is that the person's state of mind at the moment of death is what determines whether or not they become a Level 2. So it comes down to this: Does she have the type of heart that forgives or the type of heart that blames? And when you think of it that way, it's not even a question."

He was absolutely right. Before I could reply, we were interrupted.

"I hope you guys don't mind, but I brought a friend," Natalie said as she walked up with Liberty.

"Not at all!" I replied, happy to see him. He gave me

a hug and then did the whole fist bump, handshake thing with the boys.

"We can use the help," I continued. "I've already done this tour twice and come up empty both times."

Left unsaid was the full reason he was with her. He'd been protecting her in the one place we couldn't. Every day when Natalie went underground into Dead City to recharge her energy levels, Liberty went with her.

"So what brings us to the Battery?" he asked.

"This," I said, handing him the envelope. "It came addressed to me and contained a map of the George Washington walking tour and a note."

He pulled out the note and read it aloud.

"'Reserve a place in history.'"

He looked up at us and asked, "What does that even mean?"

"I wish I knew," I replied. "I thought maybe I needed to reserve a spot on an official tour of the locations, but there isn't one. Then I looked into getting reservations at different places along the route, but that didn't lead anywhere. So basically I'm stumped."

"That's why we're here," Natalie said, taking charge. "With four really smart people working together, we should be able to figure it out."

"You know there are five of us, right?" said Alex.

"I know," she said as she put an arm around him. "I'm sure you'll help too."

I absolutely loved the fact that they were able to joke the same as always. It was a sign their friendship was strong no matter what. That same relaxed mood continued as we followed the map from the Battery up to Bowling Green Park. I acted as tour guide, since I'd already walked it twice before and because I had been reading up on New York during the Revolution ever since I got the assignment months earlier.

"This is where they used to have a statue of King George III riding a horse," I said as we entered the park. "And don't ask me which way the horse's rear end was facing."

Natalie and Liberty exchanged confused looks, but I didn't bother to explain. Instead I told them a story that I'd learned in the history book about the city during the Revolution.

"Washington and his troops were in Manhattan when the Declaration of Independence was signed. And after he had it read to the troops and the local citizens, a bunch of people came here to the park, toppled the statue, and melted it down."

"What did they do with it after they melted it?" asked Natalie.

"They made it into forty thousand musket balls for the Continental Army."

"Hey, maybe that's what Marek's doing with all of that Tungsten he's melting down," Grayson said. "Turning it into musket balls."

"Is that what you think he's doing?" asked Natalie. "Melting it?"

"I know he is," Grayson responded. "I've gone through all the files that Beth got on the flash drive and can track all of the shipments from the moment he buys it up until he melts it."

"And then?" asked Alex.

"And then . . . nothing," said Grayson. "He just buys it and melts it down. I can't find any record of what he does with it after that. I don't know if he's turning it into something or if he's just storing it to use later."

Grayson was down. Despite his lighthearted observations about the Statue of Liberty, he'd been in a funk for a while. First he was upset that he hadn't been more "heroic" (his words not mine) during the fight on New Year's. Then Natalie had to rescue him when the cop from the Dead Squad was trying to throw him off the Chrysler Building. And now he was struggling to solve what was going on with Empire State Tungsten, even though he had tons of data. He felt like he wasn't helping the team at all, even though we all knew that wasn't the case.

"If anyone can figure it out, it's you," I said, trying to boost his morale.

"This conversation has gotten me hungry for cheeseburgers," Alex said. "Did George Washington have a favorite cheeseburger joint?"

Natalie stopped and looked at him. "In what way did this conversation make you think of cheeseburgers?"

"Melted statue, melted cheese," he explained, incredulous. "It's kind of obvious."

"Only to you," she said.

"Maybe," I added. "But a cheeseburger does sound really good."

We took a break from the walking tour and found a burger place that was just greasy enough to be delicious. This was also important for Natalie and Liberty because, while the undead crave different tastes than us, they do like greasy foods. We all crowded around a table as we ate our burgers and shared a couple large orders of fries.

"So do you suppose old George liked burgers?" asked Alex right before he took a big chomp out of his.

"We can check," I said. "One of his favorite places to

eat is still open over on Pearl Street. It's also where the Sons of Liberty held their secret meetings."

"I didn't know you had any sons," Natalie joked to Liberty.

"Neither did I," he replied.

"The Sons of Liberty were a secret society of patriots," I explained. "They were the ones who toppled the statue of King George and had it melted down."

"*They* were a secret society, *we're* a secret society," Alex said. "We should call ourselves The Friends of Liberty."

Liberty looked both embarrassed and pleased. We held up our sodas in a toast and said, "The Friends of Liberty."

We continued eating, and a couple moments later Grayson was nibbling on a fry when he looked at Natalie.

"Can I ask something personal?"

Natalie shrugged. "I've been wondering when you would."

He hesitated for a moment, then asked, "How did you tell your parents?"

She chuckled for a moment and looked at Liberty before answering.

"I didn't."

"They don't know?" I asked surprised.

"They know," she said. "But I didn't tell them."

"Then who did?" asked Alex.

Natalie nodded to Liberty.

"First of all you have to remember that her parents are surgeons," he said. "They knew something was wrong with what they were reading in her medical charts and I knew that they'd have to change their whole world for her to survive. So I got my mother to come with me and we met with them in the hospital."

"And you just blurted out that Natalie was undead?" Grayson asked, incredulous.

"I was a little more subtle than that. Although, I couldn't be too subtle. At one point I performed a couple demonstrations to show them my state of undeadness," he said. "I think it was my ability to completely dislocate my fingers and snap them back into place without screaming that really convinced them."

"And then?" asked Alex.

"Then my mom came in and told them the parents' side of it all," he said.

"They came around amazingly well," Natalie said. "It's funny, because when you think of them being plastic surgeons on Fifth Avenue, you think about all the rich women who come in for facelifts and nose jobs. But every year they go down to Haiti and spend two weeks helping children and really saving lives. That's the side of them I've been seeing. I think the medical component helps. Sometimes I have to remind them that I'm their daughter and not an experiment. But they've done great."

Not only did this surprise me, but so did Alex's response. He turned to Liberty.

"Thank you for looking out for her," he said. "I really am proud to be a Friend of Liberty."

Liberty smiled.

All That Glitters

After we ate, we resumed our tour and continued on to Trinity Church and St. Paul's Chapel. Trinity is where some Revolutionary War heroes like Alexander Hamilton are buried, and St. Paul's is where Washington went to church every Sunday when he was President. (New York City was the capital back then.)

"What does any of this have to do with reserving a place in history?" Grayson asked, trying to solve the mystery of the note.

"Think about what the word means," Natalie suggested. "How can you reserve something if it's already happened?"

"I know what it could be," Alex said, getting our hopes up. "Molly said that the tavern where George Washington liked to eat is still operating. Maybe we need to make a reservation there. Oooh, we can eat dinner there tonight. I could use a good meal."

"Seriously? You're already thinking about dinner?" Natalie said. "You just ate. You still have a little burger juice on your chin."

"I can't help it," he complained. "You guys keep bringing up food."

"Actually," she said, "you're the only one who's bringing up food."

"About his idea, though," I said. "You can make reservations there. It's called the Fraunces Tavern and it's a museum and a restaurant. They serve old-style food from the Colonial era. That might be the solution."

"You see?" Alex said to Natalie. "You're welcome."

"We'll look into it," she said begrudgingly, "but let's keep on with the tour for now."

Our next stop was Federal Hall. When the United States began, New York was the capital and Federal Hall was where George Washington took the oath of office as the first president. We were walking down Nassau Street toward the building when I pointed something out to the others.

"This street is where my anonymous letters supposedly came from," I said.

"What do you mean?" asked Grayson.

"Both envelopes had a return address on Nassau Street."

"Did you try to find it?" asked Grayson.

"No, that never occurred to me," I said, giving him the stink eye. "Of course I did. But it's phony. It doesn't make any sense."

I handed him the envelope and he read it aloud. "356852 Nassau Street."

"See what I mean? It's way too high a number to be an actual address," I explained. "The longest addresses on Nassau are only three digits."

"Maybe it's the number of an office in one of these buildings," Natalie said. "If we can find the office, we can find the answer."

"Nope," Liberty said, interrupting. "It's not an address and it's not an office."

I stopped and gave him a look too. "How do you know that?"

"Because it's my name," he said with a cheesy smile.

Now I was even more confused.

"It was one of the first things I memorized when I

learned the Omega code," he said. "3, 5, 68, 52 is lithium, boron, erbium, tellurium. Li, B, Er, Te, that spells Liberte. It's the French spelling, but still the best way to spell my name in the code."

I couldn't believe I hadn't figured that out. "How did I miss that?" I said, taking the envelope and looking down at it. "It's as plain as day."

"No it's not," said Alex. "The numbers aren't split, so you don't know if they're one digit or two. And it's not part of any other coded material. I wouldn't have thought it was code if I saw it."

"But if it is code, that's huge," said Natalie. "That means 'liberty' is part of the clue."

"It could be the Statue of Liberty," suggested Grayson. "Does Nassau Street run all the way?"

"Yes," said Alex. "But you have to take a submarine for the part that goes under New York Harbor."

Grayson rolled his eyes. "I meant does it run all the way to Battery Park, where we were looking at the statue earlier this morning. Maybe if you stand there on the street and look at the statue it all lines up and makes sense."

"No," I said. "Nassau only goes to Wall Street. There's no way you could see the statue from there."

"It could be the Sons of Liberty," Alex said. "You said

they used to meet at the Fraunces Tavern. That gets back to that whole reserve a place in history thing."

"That's good," Liberty said. "That makes a lot of sense."

"Let me see the note again," Natalie said, a hint of excitement in her voice.

I handed it to her and she held it up so that the sunlight shined through the paper. She looked at it for a second and smiled.

"There's a comma," she said, her excitement building. "It's faint but it's definitely there."

"A comma? That's why you made the big smiley face?" Alex said. "Because there's a comma?"

"Don't you see, Alex," she replied, playing up the moment. "A comma changes everything."

"I think it's safe to say that none of us see that," he answered. "How does a comma change everything?"

"Because without a comma in the sentence 'Reserve a place in history,' 'reserve' is a verb," she said. "That's what we've been trying to figure out. How you can make a reservation. But if there is a comma, as in 'Reserve, comma, a place in history,' then 'reserve' is a noun, an actual place in history."

And that's when I realized where we were standing.

"You are a total genius!" I said.

She flashed a grin. "I know, but don't get discouraged. I had to develop the skills."

"Okay," Alex said. "For us mere mortals, do you want to explain?"

"Look where we are," I said. "It's the Federal Reserve."

Sure enough, we were standing right next to the Federal Reserve Bank of New York.

"This is the Reserve! It's a place in history." I continued, thrilled that we'd finally figured it out.

"And check out the address," added Natalie. "We are at the intersection of Nassau Street and . . ."

We all looked up at the street sign and smiled.

It was Liberty.

"This must be where Marek is getting his money," I said as we stood looking up at the massive Federal Reserve Bank. "Remember what Milton said, the money is the key to everything."

"I don't know," said Grayson. "It's not that kind of bank. The Federal Reserve isn't for people to use. It's for giant banks and the governments of countries to use. Marek's not a country. He can't just go in and open an account or take out a loan."

"Yes, but that's not all it is," said Alex. "The Federal Reserve is also home to the world's largest . . ."

He stopped midsentence and left us hanging.

". . . never mind."

"Never mind?! The world's largest what?" asked Natalie.

"Four really smart people and me," he said, referring to her joke from earlier. "I'd hate to embarrass you all by solving the big mystery. I'll just go lift weights and eat cheeseburgers until you geniuses figure it out."

"Okay, okay, okay," she said with exaggerated emphasis. "I was joking and I'm sorry. *Five* really smart people."

"How about four really smart people and one Albert Einstein level supergenius?"

She gave him a look. "You're pushing it."

"Okay, five really smart people will do. As I was saying, the Federal Reserve isn't just a bank. It's also home to the world's largest gold deposit." The mention of gold caught our attention and Alex took a dramatic pause before he continued. "Almost a quarter of the world's gold is in the basement of that building."

"That's a lot," Natalie said, laughing. "That's a whole lot."

"Yeah, but I'm pretty sure they keep it locked up tight," said Liberty. "How would he even get in to see it, much less have access to it?"

"That's the best part," said Alex. "They give tours. I saw a documentary about it on television."

"I think we should take that tour," Natalie said as she started walking toward the entrance. "By the way, super-geniuses don't sit around watching TV."

"It was a documentary," Alex corrected as we all followed her. "Supergeniuses watch documentaries."

Considering what's inside, it's no surprise that we had to go through some major security hurdles just to get into the building. It took about twenty minutes to make it through the first wave of armed guards, metal detectors, and bag searches. At one point I think they took our pictures and ran them through facial recognition software, but I couldn't tell for sure because it was all kind of top secret-y and they weren't exactly talkative.

Finally, we made it to the end of the line. There was a woman at the counter in a crisp blue uniform with her hair pulled back tight in a bun. She wasn't what you'd call friendly.

"Tickets?"

That's all she said. Unfortunately, we didn't know what she was talking about. Natalie was in front, so she took the lead. "How much are they?"

"They're free."

"Great," she said. "We'll take five."

"No," the woman corrected. "You must already have them.

Tickets are ordered online at least one month in advance."

"Well," Natalie said, trying to charm her a little. "Since we're here and have already gone through the security line . . . and since they're free . . . is there any way we can get them now?"

"No."

Alex started to try a follow-up but it was obvious Ms. Single Syllable wasn't going to change her mind. Luckily, her supervisor was a little nicer. He was older, his hair and moustache on the silver side of gray, and his smile was welcoming.

"What seems to be the problem?" he asked as he walked up behind her.

"No tickets," she explained curtly.

He looked at us for a moment, and I used my best pleading eyes. We all did.

"Wait a second, I think they're part of that school group from Texas," he said as he winked at Natalie. "Isn't that right? Aren't you from Texas?"

"Yee haw," said Natalie with a drawl. "We sure are."

Before the woman could protest, the supervisor told her that he'd watch the counter for fifteen minutes so she could take a break. That took care of her, and once she was gone, he turned to us and asked, "You're not going to make me regret this, are you?"

"No, sir," we said in unison.

He smiled and handed each one of us a ticket and directed us to join a group of sixth-graders who were wearing matching purple MANSFIELD TAKES MANHATTAN T-shirts.

"Yee haw?" I said to Natalie as we walked over.

She shrugged and laughed. "It was the best I could think of."

We had to wait about ten minutes for the tour to begin, so we bonded with the school group. And by "bonded," I mean all their girls looked dreamily at Alex while Natalie and I helped their teachers with directions to their next stop. Finally, a tour guide came out and led us toward the vault.

"Welcome to the Federal Reserve Bank of New York's gold vault," he said, his Brooklyn accent making it sound like there was a *w* in the middle of "vault." "It holds more than half a million gold bars, weighing approximately 6,700 tons."

It took Grayson less than thirty seconds to say, "That's over $380 billion. Billion with a *b*."

The guard stopped and smiled. "Very good math. $382 billion to be exact."

I don't know which impressed me more: the money or Grayson's math skills.

"All of the gold in the vault belongs to foreign countries," he continued. "Much of it came here around World War II, when European governments wanted to make sure that their money was secure."

As he talked, he led us through a series of massive steel doors, past many more armed guards, and finally to a long hallway where the gold is held. It's kept in blue cages with numbers and multiple padlocks on the doors. He talked about the meticulous way in which each bar is tracked, measured, weighed, and reweighed.

"Now I have a question for you," the man said as he looked out at us. "We are eighty feet below ground and there is one important thing that makes this gold vault possible. Does anyone know what it is?"

He looked first at all the kids in the school group, but they just shook their heads. Then he looked at us. We were equally stumped until Natalie came up with the answer.

"Manhattan schist?"

He smiled. "What a smart group this is. Good with math, good with geology. Manhattan schist is exactly right. If it weren't for New York's superstrong bedrock, this vault could not exist, because the weight of the gold would cause it to sink deeper into the ground."

We all exchanged looks at the mention of Manhattan schist. Everything was tantalizingly close to coming together. As for the tour, it was interesting and the gold was impressive, but it seemed like the Federal Reserve might be a dead end. For the life of us, we couldn't figure out how Marek could get so much as a single bar out of the vault. There were too many safety measures. And even if he could steal some, any missing gold would be noticed within forty-eight hours.

"It's impossible," Natalie said as we walked around the museum exhibit at the end of the tour. The exhibit had archival pictures, old scales, and equipment used for measuring the gold. There was even a mountain of shredded cash. (Shredding old bills is one of the things the bank is in charge of doing.) "With the gates and the vaults and the many people with big guns, I don't see how he could get any of it."

"It's not like he can come in at night, either," Grayson said, motioning to a display about the massive vault door. "The only way into that vault is through a ninety-ton steel door that is locked air-tight every night. In fact, it's shut so tightly that one time a paper clip got in the door and shut the entire system down. There's no getting through it."

"Then why do I still think that it's exactly what he's doing?" I asked.

"Because it's Marek," said Natalie. "And he always seems to figure out how to pull off the impossible."

"Check it out," Alex called to us.

We walked over to where he and Liberty were looking at a display featuring a timeline of the building's construction.

"This is the vault being built in the early 1920s," he said, pointing at a large brown-tinted photo of the construction crew hard at work. "They're eighty feet underground, blasting their way through the Manhattan schist."

"Okay," said Natalie. "Why is that important?"

"Look at the man in charge." Alex pointed to a man in a hardhat. We recognized him instantly.

"Marek Blackwell," said Grayson.

"It makes sense," said Liberty. "Marek worked underground for almost a century. He worked on a lot of the big projects."

"And he wasn't alone," said Grayson, pointing to another face.

I expected to see that it was another of the Unlucky 13. But it wasn't. Still, it was a face that we all recognized.

"Is that the guard?" asked Alex. "The one who let us in without the tickets?"

We looked closely, and one by one came to the conclusion that it was in fact the guard. His hair and moustache were darker, but there was no denying who it was.

"You think he's friends with Marek?" asked Grayson.

"If he is, then why did he help us?" I asked. "You'd think we'd be the last people he'd help.

Natalie had a look of concern. "Maybe he didn't help us. Maybe he put us on that tour so he'd know where we'd be for the next hour."

"Why?" I asked, still not getting it.

"So he'd have time to call in reinforcements," she said.

We looked toward the exit. There was only one way out of the building. We looked back at the guard station, but the supervisor was no longer there.

"So you think he recognized us, made sure we got in, and then called his friends?" asked Alex.

"That's exactly what I think," she replied. "It's brilliant. There's only one way in and out. The street's narrow, so we don't have a lot of options. It's the perfect place to set a trap."

We all nodded in agreement and looked to the door. We didn't have a lot of options. We were going to have to go out and face whatever was there. Marek's war was about to begin.

Trinity

So what do you guys think?" asked Natalie as we looked out toward the doorway that exited onto Liberty Street. "Are they out there waiting for us?"

"My guess is yes," said Grayson.

"Mine too," I added.

"Maybe we should just fight them," suggested Alex. "We know they're going to attack at some point, maybe we should just stand tall and fight back now."

I didn't like this idea at all. "There are only five of us," I said. "They'll have us outnumbered, and probably by a lot."

"That's what happened to George Washington, isn't

it?" Grayson asked me. "You've been studying the Revolutionary War, what did he do when the British had him outnumbered?"

"When he realized he couldn't win, he escaped instead," I said. "The British had him trapped in Brooklyn and he got away right from under their noses by sneaking his troops across the river in the middle of the night. By the time the redcoats woke up and realized what had happened, it was too late."

"I think that's what we should do too," said Natalie. "We've got to figure out a way to sneak out of here."

"Okay, but we won't be able to wait until the middle of the night like Washington did," Alex said. "So we're not going to be able to hide in the dark."

"True," she said with a smile. "But we can hide in the sixth grade."

She nodded toward all the purple-shirted sixth graders who were mobbed together about to leave. There was another group in addition to the ones who were with us on the tour, so there were about forty of them all together.

"You think we can blend in with them?" Liberty asked. "They're all wearing matching shirts and we're not."

"True, but all we have to do is blend in long enough to

make it to the corner," she said. "Once we're that far, we can make a run for it."

"Just like George did," I added.

Alex thought it over and nodded. "I like it. But we need a plan for where we go once we make it to the corner. This should give us a head start, but they're going to chase after us."

"I don't think the subway's safe," Natalie said. "It's too easy to get slowed down waiting for a train."

"Besides," Grayson added, "the subway's kind of their home turf."

"I have an idea," I said cautiously. "But it will only work if we can make it to Trinity Church."

The school group started moving toward the door, so there wasn't really any time for me to explain it.

"I vote Trinity Church," Natalie said.

"Agreed," said the others.

I felt a lump in my throat and said a silent prayer that my plan would actually work. Lately it felt like most of them hadn't.

The school group was like a floating blob as it worked its way out the door, and we tried to mix in and spread out so we didn't draw attention to ourselves. Some of the kids recognized us and started up conversations, which helped us blend in a little more.

"Keep your eyes down and faces covered as much as you can," Natalie whispered to Grayson and me as she walked passed us. "Until we make it to the corner."

We caught our first break when we stepped outside and saw two tour buses dropping people off. The buses helped us hide, because they blocked the view of the sidewalk we were on.

"I see four bad guys directly across the street," Alex said in a low voice. "They're still watching the door. I don't think they noticed us."

"There's another pair back behind us by the pretzel vendor," added Natalie. "I saw their reflection in the windshield of the tour bus."

We knew there were at least six of them there for us, but so far none of them seemed to be aware that we'd exited the building. We were almost to the corner when one of the teachers spoke up.

"All right, Mansfield, everybody line up!" she called out to the school kids. "We need to do a head count."

The students started lining up alongside the building, and there was no way we could stay with them without really sticking out, so we had to keep walking.

"Pick up the pace," said Liberty, who was behind me.

"Three on the opposite corner," said Grayson, turning

his face down and away from them. It seemed like the undead were everywhere.

We were almost to Nassau Street when I made eye contact with none other than my favorite Dead Squad member. It was one-eared Officer Pell, standing directly in front of us. He seemed surprised that we'd gotten that far without anyone noticing, but pleased nonetheless to see me.

"Hello, Molly," he said with a raspy hiss as he moved right toward me. He reached out to grab me by the shoulder, but out of nowhere Alex clocked him with a punch across the jaw that knocked him down flat. Just like that three more zombies noticed us and leapt out.

Our head start wouldn't mean anything if we couldn't get past them in a hurry. In a flash I took out one at the knee, Natalie knocked down another with a crack of her elbow against his jaw, and Liberty did a nifty move when the last one tried to punch him. He spun around like a dancer and managed to stomp on the back of his calf, snapping his leg bone in half. They weren't down for good, but we had our opening and we burst out into a full sprint.

We caught some luck when the traffic light changed just as we reached the corner, so that we didn't even have to break stride as we bolted toward the church two blocks away. My pulse quickened as we ran, in part because of the excitement but even more out of nervousness. The others were counting on my plan working. I couldn't mess up again.

It took about two and a half minutes until we were running up to the iron gate that marks the entrance of the church. When we reached it, we stopped for a second to take a quick breath and to look back over our shoulders.

"I don't see anyone," said Grayson.

"You don't see them," Liberty said, "but they're there. I guarantee it."

"It's all you," Natalie said to me. "Save the day."

"Follow me," I instructed them confidently. "I've got this."

Trinity is a beautiful gothic church that I'm sure was impressive when it first opened, but now it's dwarfed by skyscrapers on all sides. The churchyard serves as a cemetery and has many famous early American heroes buried in it. When you add up all the tourists and the tombstones, it's a crowded place to be in a hurry. We tried to be respectful without being slow.

I led the others inside the church and down a stairway to a basement vault. Crypts lined the walls and marble markers signified who was buried in them. This was my first time coming down here, so I hoped that I had my facts right.

I turned a corner, worried that we might run into a dead end, but was relieved to see another set of stairs descending farther down.

"Is anyone following us?" Natalie asked.

Alex looked back as we turned the corner. "Not that I can see."

The stairwell emptied out into a darker crypt. The tombstones on the wall in here dated back to the late 1600s.

"This is the oldest part of the church," I said. "We're almost there."

We entered the final vault, and there, in addition to the crypts, was a small construction area in the corner marked off with bright orange tape and thick layers of plastic sheeting. I got down on my hands and knees and pulled up the bottom of the plastic.

"In here," I said as I crawled under.

The others followed, and when we came up on the other side we were in a sub-basement with a dirt floor. It was only about four feet high, so we had to sort of walk and crawl half bent over in between the brick pilings that held up the building.

"There it is," I said, pointing toward an old stone doorway that had been dug out. Carved into the keystone at the top of the entry was the phrase TUTUS LOCUS.

"What is *tutus locus*?" asked Natalie.

"It's Latin," said Grayson. "It means 'safe passage'."

"That's right," I told them. "The Sons of Liberty built this during the Revolution. They would have their meetings in the church, and if the redcoats came, they'd escape through here. It was used again during the Civil War as part of the Underground Railroad."

"Then how come we've never heard of it?" asked Alex.

"Because it was lost and forgotten for more than 125 years," I explained. "It was just rediscovered a few months ago."

"Where does it lead?" asked Natalie.

"Away from the Dead Squad," I answered.

She smiled. "That's good enough for me."

We passed through the doorway and entered a centuries-old tunnel lined with brick walls. There was absolutely no light, so we took turns illuminating the way with our phones. It was hot and sweaty, and my face was caked with dirt and dust. After about fifteen minutes we stopped to catch our breaths and to listen for any Dead Squad members who may have figured it out and followed us down here.

"I don't hear anything," Natalie said happily after about thirty seconds of silence. "Except maybe a couple of rats in the distance."

"Speaking of rodents," Alex said, "let's hear it for our one and only Gopher."

They all did quiet little golf claps and tried to fist-bump me in the dark. For the first time I didn't mind the nickname. (Well, not much anyway.)

"How did you find out about this place, anyway?" Grayson asked. "You said it was just discovered a few months ago?"

"That's right," I answered. "The professor at CCNY, the one I've been studying, she found it in some old papers she was researching. In fact, she was arranging to lead a thorough archeological dig of the entire passageway."

"*Was* arranging?" Natalie asked. "What stopped her?"

"Marek," I answered. "Or rather, his funding. He donated a ton of money to support her research for the new George Washington book, so the excavation of the tunnel has been postponed until that's done."

"When I first put you on this assignment to study her and what she was doing, you weren't happy," said Natalie. "You thought it was going to be boring and that I was punishing you."

"You could tell that?" I said, thinking that I had kept my emotions hidden.

"I could tell," she said. "But, this is why. None of us would have read it carefully enough to find this and remember it when we needed it most."

After more than a few mistakes, it felt good to get something right.

"All right," Alex said. "We better keep following this thing until we can find a safe way back up to the surface."

We started walking again, although not as rushed as before.

"You'd think that studying this tunnel would be more important than her book on Washington," Grayson said. "I wonder why she didn't do this first and then write the book later."

"That's back to Marek," I replied. "His financial support specified that the book had to come first and then this."

"He's really weird, isn't he?" said Alex.

"Usually I've found him to be more smart than weird," Liberty said. "There's always a reason for what he does. Even if we don't always see it right away."

A couple minutes later we reached a junction where the tunnel joined up with another one that was bigger. It was the underground equivalent of going from a side street to a major road. It was about ten feet by ten feet and there was even a little light.

"Wait a second," Liberty said as he rapped the walls and the ceiling with his knuckles. "It's all wood."

"Is that important?" asked Alex.

"Have you ever been in an all-wooden tunnel before?"

Alex shrugged. "I guess not."

"I think this may be a cattle tunnel," Liberty said. "I've heard about them, but I didn't know if they were real or it was just a legend."

"What's a cattle tunnel?" asked Natalie.

"Back before refrigeration they needed to bring the cattle from the boats on the river to the slaughterhouses in the Meat-packing District," Liberty said. "They couldn't risk them stampeding down the streets of New York, so they drove them through underground tunnels made out of wood. They had cowboys and everything."

"Are you being serious?" I asked.

"Totally," he said. "When they stopped needing them, the tunnels were built over and people lost track of where they are."

"That means this should take us out to the river if we go that way," Alex said pointing to the left.

We all started that way but stopped a few moments later when we heard a squeaking noise coming toward us.

"I hope it's not ghost cows," joked Grayson.

"Whatever it is, we don't want to come face to face with it," said Natalie. "Let's get back in the other tunnel."

"You mean the dark and dirty one?" I asked.

"No, I mean the safe one," corrected Natalie.

"Good point."

We hurried back to the other tunnel and disappeared into the darkness. Then we watched to see who was coming.

The creaking got louder and louder, and soon we could tell it was the sound of metal wheels going over the wooden floor. Every now and then there was a little conversation between two people, although we couldn't make it out.

Finally we saw two men, big strong Level 2s, dressed almost like miners with hardhats and lights. They were pulling an old metal flatbed cart, one of its wheels squeaking with every rotation. And even though it was dark, the cargo was bright and impossible to miss.

Six shining gold bars.

Wolfram

We sat quietly in the tunnel until the two men and their cargo were long gone. Other than the steady squeak, squeak, squeak of their wheels fading in the distance, there was no other sound except for the occasional deep breath as we considered the magnitude of what we'd just seen. We crawled out and back into the cattle tunnel.

"Okay, Mr. Math," Natalie said, turning to Grayson. "How much are we talking about there?"

"Let's see," he said. "According to what they told us on the tour each bar weighs twenty-seven pounds. That's about $640,000 per bar. Multiply that by six bars and they were carrying around 3.8 million dollars in gold."

"Why are two L2s moving nearly four million dollars in gold?" asked Alex.

"I imagine they're stealing it," Natalie said.

"You'd think that," answered Alex. "But they're walking toward the gold vault, not away from it. They were coming from the river."

"Should we follow them?" I asked.

Natalie shook her head. "No, that's way too risky. I think we need to get back to the surface and get home."

"Home sounds good," Grayson said.

Alex's sense of direction was right on. After about fifteen minutes of walking, the tunnel dumped us out next to the Hudson River.

"This must have been where the cows were unloaded from the boats," said Liberty.

"Mmmm, that makes me think of hamburgers," said Alex.

Natalie laughed. "Everything makes you think of hamburgers."

"That's not true," he replied. "Little Italy makes me think of lasagna."

"Okay," she said. "Everything makes you think of food."

Alex thought about this. "That's probably true."

We were covered in dirt, dust, and sweat, but it felt good. We'd managed to escape the Dead Squad's trap and I'd played a big part in that. We also knew that Marek was doing something with the gold from the Federal Reserve.

"I'll get word to your mother about what we found and see what she wants us to do next," Liberty said.

I was jealous that he had more access to Mom than I did, but I understood. "Great," I said.

"Let's get home and get some rest," Natalie said. "Good job, everyone."

"Especially you, Gopher," Alex said with a wink.

The others headed uptown while Grayson and I went south toward Battery Park, which is where the morning began. I could tell he was feeling down and wanted someone to talk to.

"My dad's working late tonight and my sister's out with friends," I said. "Mind if I come hang out with you?"

"That'd be great," he said.

We took the subway to Fort Greene and walked toward Grayson's neighborhood. After a few minutes without either of us saying a word, he looked up at me, his eyes red.

"I'm quitting," he said.

"Quitting what?" I asked.

"Omega."

"You can't."

"I'm holding everyone back," he said. "You've got Liberty. You've got Beth. They're not even part of the team but they do more to help than I do."

There was a bench on the edge of the park and we sat down there.

"I don't get it," I said. "You're so important to everything we're doing. You're . . . essential."

He laughed. "For someone who is so good at seeing things that are hidden, how can you possibly miss something so obvious? It happened again today. We got attacked on the corner and everybody took someone out but me."

"Yes, but . . ."

"And at the Chrysler Building everyone was great . . . but me. Even Beth, who minutes earlier didn't even know that the undead existed, fought like a pro. Me? I would have been thrown off the Chrysler Building if Natalie hadn't come back."

His face was pained and heartbroken. I knew that Omega meant as much to him as it did to me. This was really hard for him.

"We all help in different ways," I tried to explain.

"That's a nice way of saying I can't fight," he replied.

"Do you know I've never killed one? In two years I've never once killed a zombie. And on New Year's Eve, I was the one fighting Edmund first. I didn't even slow him down, which is why he was able to do that to Natalie. It is one hundred percent my fault that she is undead."

"That's absolutely not true," I told him. "Believe me, because I think it's one hundred percent my fault. You are so valuable to this team, Grayson. You have to see that. I understand why you're upset, but you can't leave us. We need you."

"I can't even figure out why the tungsten's important, and I've spent months on it. I've studied their records. I've researched geology books. And I'm stumped."

"Let's solve it right now," I said. "Tell me everything you know about tungsten."

"There's too much to even tell."

"Just start talking," I said. "What are the basics?"

"Tungsten is a rare, hard metal most often found in Canada, China, and Russia," he said. "It's gray and shiny. It's used as the filament in lightbulbs and X-ray tubes, none of which have anything to do with Marek."

"Forget trying to connect it to Marek," I said. "Just keep telling me about tungsten. It starts with a *T* but its chemical symbol is *W*. What's that about?"

"It comes from the Swedish word *wolfram*," he said. "Tungsten's chemical number is seventy-four. Its standard atomic weight is 183.84 and its density is 19.25 grams per centimeter cubed."

And that's where he stopped.

The eyes that were red with tears suddenly turned bright.

"That's it," he said. "That's how he's doing it."

I smiled along with him and said, "You know I have absolutely no idea what you're talking about, right? You know this is exactly why I said we needed you?"

He looked at me, the white of his teeth appearing brighter than usual because of the remnants of dirt and dust on his face.

"It's *exactly* the same as gold," he said. "Tungsten's density and its properties are identical to gold. That's what he's doing. He's swapping the tungsten with the gold in the Federal Reserve!"

Back to School

I don't know how you go to school here," Beth said as we walked across the campus. "It looks like it belongs in a horror movie."

She had a point. Once the home of a notorious mental hospital, MIST's gothic architecture was scary enough on bright sunny days. But a fast-approaching storm had filled the sky with dark clouds, and the first week of summer vacation had given the school a certain level of abandoned eeriness.

"Believe it or not, you get used to it," I said as I typed a code into a keypad by the door to the library.

"What's the code?" she asked.

I thought I'd give her a chance to test her code-breaking skills. "3, 35, 18, 39."

"Lithium, bromine, argon, yttrium," she replied. "Li, Br, Ar, Y. Library. That's easy enough."

Just as we had that first day beneath CCNY, our Omega team was arriving separately. We walked through the library without turning on any lights, navigating the stacks and the bookcases quickly. We took the stairs down to special collections, where the air had the scent of dust and old literature.

"Look at those girls!"

We looked across the room to see Mom waiting for us. The security light over her head gave her a slight green haze.

"I miss you two so much."

She came over and hugged us, and before the others arrived we spent a few minutes talking about mundane things like our plans for the summer and the particulars of Beth's job at the drama camp. Those are the details that meant the most to her, the little things that filled in the pictures of our lives.

Alex and Grayson joined us a few minutes later. And a few minutes after that Natalie arrived with Liberty.

"So I hear you guys have been busy," Mom said.

"Let's see if we can figure out what to do next."

She led us back through the special collections to a small reading room. It looked like something you'd find in an old English manor, with a pair of overstuffed chairs, floor to ceiling oak bookcases, and even a fireplace. Without hesitating she walked right up to the fireplace, ducked down, and entered it. She pushed on the brick wall in the back and it opened up onto a staircase.

"This way," she said, directing us down the staircase.

This led us to a cozy studio apartment that had a similar vibe as the reading room. There were bookcases and books everywhere.

"Welcome to my home," said Milton Blackwell as he greeted each one of us with a hearty handshake.

"I thought your home was the lab underneath CCNY," I said.

He laughed. "When you're over 140 years old, you get to have more than one. That's more my home to work and this is more my home to relax and think. It's where I lived the whole time I was principal of MIST. I like it because it keeps me close to school and because it comes with a fully-stocked library upstairs."

We all settled down on comfortable couches, and he poured us hot tea and served cookies.

"Liberty filled us in on most of what you've learned, but we wanted to get everybody together," Mom said. "Let's go around the room and try to paint a full picture of what Marek's up to."

"First of all, he's stealing hundreds of millions of dollars from the Federal Reserve Bank," Grayson said. "He was part of the construction team that built the vault back in the 1920s and he must have left some sort of back door entrance that cuts through the Manhattan schist. All the security is focused on protecting it from above ground. No one would have thought you could come from underneath."

"That's not even the brilliant part," said Alex. "Tell him how he's beating all the checks and balances."

"He's swapping the gold bars a few at a time with bars made out of tungsten and coated with a layer of gold."

Milton's head bobbed up and down as he did some mental calculations. "That *is* brilliant. Their properties are almost identical. They'd pass a lot of tests."

"That's exactly right," said Grayson.

"How does this involve the historian from CCNY?" asked Mom.

"She uncovered a secret tunnel the Sons of Liberty

built during the Revolutionary War," I explained. "She was planning to excavate and study it. If she did that, she would have found the old cattle tunnels Marek is using to move his tungsten and gold. By paying her to do something else, he protected his secret."

"I think there may be more to it than that," Natalie said. "Molly was explaining how the forts were arranged on Manhattan during the Revolution. This professor is an expert in that and I think Marek is trying to borrow that knowledge."

This was a new revelation to me.

"How?" I asked.

"I saw it last night," she said. "I was looking at a map of all the RUNY construction sites and I noticed it looked a lot like the map you showed me of the Revolutionary War forts. The layout is the same."

"I don't get it," said Liberty.

"I don't think he's building entertainment centers underground," she said. "I think that's what they'll look like."

"But they'll really be forts," I said, getting her point.

"Think about it," she said. "He has hundreds of millions of dollars to build underground forts and arm an undead army."

"This is freaky stuff," Beth said. "How are we going to stop him?"

"We may not have to," Alex said. "The Dead Squad changed the frequency of their communication channel after our little battle at the Chrysler Building, but after some searching I found the new one and have been able to listen in on their conversations for the last couple days. They don't talk as much as they used to, but I can tell one thing for sure. Marek is sick."

"That's what we understand too," Mom said.

"His body is rejecting most of the transplants," Alex replied. "And they are searching for the two of you around the clock."

"Why are they looking for Mom and Milton?" asked Beth. "What do they have to do with Marek being sick?"

There was a slight pause in the conversation, and then Milton answered, "My brother needs my body parts in order to survive."

Beth's eyes opened wide. She went to say something, but she couldn't make the words.

"We know," I said. "It's beyond gross."

Everyone was silent for a minute, then I shook my head and went on. "He may be sick," I said. "But he's making a public appearance tomorrow."

"Where?" asked Mom.

"The Central Park Zoo," I said. "I got another letter yesterday."

I handed the envelope to my mother. Inside there was a map of the Central Park Zoo and a press release that said Marek Blackwell was going to break ground on construction for a new exhibit at the zoo. There was also a note, which Mom read aloud.

"When Marek makes his announcement, everything will be clear."

"Scary, huh?" I said.

"Yes," replied my mother.

"It has shades of New Year's Eve," added Alex. "We go expecting one announcement, and it turns out to be something else."

"I know," I answered. "That's why I don't want to make any recommendation about what we should do. I just thought I should share it with all of you."

"First of all, what happened on New Year's wasn't your fault," said Natalie. "And secondly, you know what we have to do."

"She's right," said Mom. "We have to be there."

24

Groundbreaking Development

I t was a beautiful June day and crowds packed the Central Park Zoo. There were seven of us there. Alex, Beth, and I were together near the sea lion exhibit while Natalie, Grayson, and Liberty were over by the snow monkeys. My mom was the wildcard; she was taking advantage of the fact that you can look into the zoo from the walkway that runs through the park. She blended in with the tourists hanging out by the Delacorte Clock.

None of us were next to the penguins, which is where Marek was making his announcement. We wanted to be close enough to see and hear what was going on but not where he'd be likely to see us. Although we were somewhat exposed, we felt comfortable that the undead weren't going to attack us in front of a bunch of kids on summer vacation at the zoo. Marek was building a new reputation as a civic leader and couldn't let anything he was involved with become too messy.

"Anything interesting?" I asked Alex, who was listening in on the Dead Squad's communications.

"Nope," he said. "Hardly any chatter at all."

I gave him a look. "Chatter? Did you learn that reading some book about cops?"

He looked a little hurt at the dig. "That's what my uncle Paul calls it."

"I'm just kidding," I said. "I do that when I'm nervous."

"There's Mr. Evil," said Beth.

Marek Blackwell arrived with the zoo director, and the two of them approached a small podium and microphone. Like always, he was well dressed with a crisp coat and tie despite the hot June afternoon. They stood in front of a few dozen people, including some members of the press. Among them were some television news crews, including one with Brock Hampton, the local reporter who often broadcasts coded messages to the undead.

"I'd like to welcome everyone and thank you for coming," the director said into the microphone. "We are going to have a short presentation today about an exciting new addition we're adding to the zoo. Marek Blackwell has donated a very generous sum of money to support a new habitat for the penguins here at the Central Park Zoo. Today we are breaking ground on what will be a state-of-the-art facility for some of the zoo's most popular residents. I'd like to introduce Marek Blackwell."

There was applause as Marek moved to the microphone. He seemed frail and uneasy.

"I think you're right," I said to Alex. "He looks sick."

Someone handed him a gold-plated shovel, and he said, "I know a little something about digging."

This elicited polite laughter from the people in the crowd.

"I've spent most of my life under this great city, digging holes to carry everything from drinking water to subways," he continued. "And now I am reinventing underground New York, but that doesn't mean I'm not concerned about what happens up here on the surface."

There was some more laughter, and I had to admit that he had undeniable charm. It was easy to see how he got people to support him.

"When I put this shovel into the ground, it will mark the beginning of a new habitat for the zoo's penguins. It's my hope that it will be a treasure for the families of New York but also for the scientists who study these amazing animals. That means so much to me because of my brother Milton."

Alex and I exchanged looks. We had no idea what he was talking about.

"He was very special to me. But he wasn't just family, he was also a great scientist. That's why this center is so important to me, and that's why it will be named the Milton Blackwell Penguin Research Center."

More applause and more confusion on our part.

"I cannot think of a more appropriate way to honor his memory. He will be missed."

"Why is he speaking of him in the past tense like he's dead?" I asked.

I looked up at Marek, and I swear that he was looking right at me as he shook hands with well wishers and left the podium. Before I could even react, Alex grabbed me by the arm and pulled me closer to him.

"What? What?" I asked nervous.

He held up his finger to shush me for a moment while he listened to something over the radio. "They just arrested your mother."

"They what?" Beth and I said in unison.

"The call just came in over the radio," he said. "They just arrested your mother."

We looked over toward the Delacorte Clock and saw that two police officers, both with Dead Squad patches on their shoulders, had my mother handcuffed and were taking her away. Even though we were close enough to see, the railing around the zoo made it impossible for us to chase after her. We'd have to run all the way over to the entrance.

"What are they arresting her for?" I said to Alex.

"Yeah," said Beth, "what could the charge possibly be?"

"Does it matter?"

I turned to see that Marek Blackwell had now come over to us.

"You must be Beth," he said, offering his hand to my sister.

"If you think I'm shaking your hand, you're crazy," she said.

"Haven't they told you, young lady?" he said. "I'm as crazy as a loon. Or is that crazy as a fox? The fox is the one who acts crazy but gets his way. Just like I did with the letters I sent to Molly."

"You wrote them?"

He nodded. "I wanted to make sure that you were close but not too close. And then, of course, when the time was right, I needed to make sure that you brought your mother to me so that she couldn't be protecting my brother."

Now it made sense. He needed to get her away from Milton so that his men could get to him. Once again, I'd played right into his trap.

"I'm going to make the same offer to you that I made to her six months ago," he said. "We can have peace. I have no interest in fighting you or your friends. I have no interest in fighting anyone."

"What about my mother and Milton?" I demanded.

He made a sheepish expression. "I'm afraid it's too late for both of them. I need my brother for health reasons, and I need your mother because . . . well, let's just face it . . . I want her out of the picture for good. I named the Penguin habitat for Milton. I figured I owed him at least that much. I'll figure out some way to memorialize your mother, too."

I think any one of us would have killed him there on the spot, but in addition to being surrounded by the media, he was protected by four of his biggest Dead Squad members, including Officer Pell. The whole time Marek talked, Pell stared daggers at me.

"I'll be seeing you around," Pell said as he started to walk away with Marek. As he did, he threw a punch into Alex's gut. "That's for the sucker punch you threw at my jaw the other day."

They escorted Marek away, and I started hyperventilating as I tried to figure out what to do next. Natalie, Liberty, and Grayson rushed over to us.

"What just happened?" asked Natalie.

"They arrested my mom and I think they have captured Milton," I told them.

Alex was still recovering from the sucker punch, but once he got his breath back he said, "We don't know that for sure. I haven't heard anything on the radio about them getting their hands on him. But that's definitely their plan. That's why they have your mom in custody, so she can't help him."

"What are they going to do with Mom?" asked Beth. "Just take her somewhere and kill her?"

"They can't do that," said Alex. "They had to call in the arrest. That means there's a record and they have to follow procedures. My guess is that they'll keep her locked up for now and transfer her to the Tombs tonight."

"The what?" I asked.

"The Tombs," he said. "It's what they call the main city

jail. It's bad news. It would be incredibly easy for them to fake an accident in there and make it look like another prisoner killed her."

Everything seemed grim, but for some reason I was more focused than ever. I know that Natalie is our team captain, but I thought it was time for me to take charge.

"Okay, here's what we're going to do," I said. "But it's going to take all of us at the top of our game. Natalie, Alex, and Liberty, you three get over to MIST and see if you can help Milton. They have him outnumbered, but he's smart. Smarter than all of us combined. He may be able to hold them off until help arrives. Listen in on the radio so you know what the bad guys are up to."

"Got it," said Natalie, no hesitation about taking orders from me. "What are you three going to do?"

I looked at her and smiled. "We're going to break my mother out of jail."

25

Jail Birds (We Return to Where the Story Began)

The Central Garden & Sea Lion Pool is at the heart of the Central Park Zoo. It features a rocky island surrounded by water and is home to eight California sea lions. Every afternoon at one thirty an animal keeper climbs up onto the island to feed the sea lions and talk about them. It's incredibly popular, which is why the crowd was three people deep all the way around the tank.

A sea lion name Scooter was demonstrating his ability to stand up on his fore-flippers, when there was a loud gasp in the crowd.

"Mom!" cried out a young boy. "What's that girl doing?"

I was the girl, and the thing I was doing was balancing on the rail that ringed the pool. Embarrassingly, my balance was worse than Scooter's.

"Please get down from there," the keeper directed me in a forceful voice.

Despite my wobbly beginning I finally managed to stand up straight.

"It is not safe for you or the animals if you encroach upon an exhibit," he continued. "You must stay on public paths!"

Satisfied that I had everybody's attention and was the focus of more than a few video cameras, I was ready to make a splash. (Sorry, puns are a weakness of mine.) I thought it would be a good touch to shout something as I did it, and for some reason my mind went back to the Sons of Liberty and their safe passage tunnel.

"Tutus locus!"

It didn't make sense, but I thought it sounded good. And before anyone could ask me what it meant, I leapt into the air and cannonballed into the nearly freezing water. An instant shock ran through my body as I submerged for a moment of silence before I started to float back to the surface. When I came back up, it was anything but quiet.

I heard laughter, yelling, and lots of vigorous instructions from the keeper up on the rocky island.

In addition to being surprised at the water temperature, I was caught off guard by the fact that it was salt water. This should have been obvious, considering that California sea lions live off the coast of California in the Pacific Ocean, but in my mind the water looked fresh, not salty.

Two of the sea lions, I think their names were April and Clarisse, swam alongside me as I dog paddled through the water until the police arrived. As I expected, it wasn't a member of the Dead Squad that came, but instead a regular cop, a female officer named Strickland.

When she showed up on the scene, I happily swam back to the edge, climbed out of the pool, and surrendered myself to her.

I find it interesting that while the keepers and many of the mothers sneered at me like I belonged on the FBI's Most Wanted List, Officer Strickland took it all in stride.

"Try not to slide all over the seat," she said as she put me in the back of her squad car. "I'm going to have to come back out and dry it later."

"Yes, ma'am," I said. "I'm very sorry about that."

It was a short drive from the zoo to the Central Park Precinct of the NYPD. Alex had told me about the precinct, and it was actually quite pretty. In order to maintain the beauty of the park, the precinct was housed in a series of buildings that were once horse stables. Many of the structures had been built out of Manhattan schist, which is why the Dead Squad had selected it as the ideal place for their headquarters.

"Several people reported you shouting some kind of threat when you stood up on the rail," she said to me when she was writing her report. "What was it?"

"*Tutus locus,*" I said. "It's Latin for 'safe passage'."

She snickered. "And who were you threatening?"

"No one intentionally."

She stopped writing her report for a moment and looked at me. It was clear she didn't know what to make of the whole situation.

"Where do you go to school?" she asked.

"MIST," I said. "The Metropolitan Institute of Science and Technology."

"That's a prestigous school," she said. "You get good grades there?"

I nodded. "Yes, ma'am. All As."

"All As means you're smart," she said. "But what you did today was not smart."

"No, ma'am. It was stupid."

"Do you have an explanation?"

I shook my head.

"I'll tell you what I think it is," she said. "I think you had some kind of crazy idea that it would be funny, and you made a mistake."

"That's pretty accurate," I told her.

"What do your parents do?" she asked.

"Well, there's just my dad," I said. "He's a paramedic with the FDNY."

That caught her attention, which is exactly what I was hoping for. The police and fire departments were part of the same extended family, which kind of made us related.

I can't say enough about how great she was. We talked for a little while more and then she had me call my dad. He explained that he couldn't come to pick me up until his shift was over. As a bonus, while I was at her desk, I could hear the communications over the radio and knew that the Dead Squad was having trouble finding Milton.

Then she brought me here to the cell where I am right now. Like I said when I started to explain all of this, it was my intention to get arrested and wind up here. So that part of my plan worked. But for everything to work out, a lot of other pieces are going to have to fall into place.

The first is that my sister has to be able to explain every-thing to my father. Or at least, she has to explain enough to get him to play along. It's going to take a leap of faith for him to buy into the plan, but Beth can be amazingly persuasive. And Dad's always had a soft spot for his daughters. The second, harder to predict portion, is that the Dead Squad is going to have to follow police procedures, like Alex said they would.

I was hoping that Mom would be in one of the holding cells, but I don't see her anywhere. I'm trying to stay upbeat, but it isn't easy. If I've miscalculated then the only thing I've accomplished is getting locked up so that I can't help at all.

I look across the squad room and notice that there's some activity in one of the interrogation rooms. Finally, the door opens and I see Mom in handcuffs being led out of the room. I turn my back to them so that the two Dead Squadders can't see my face. They lock her into the cell right next to mine.

"You're going to wait here for a little bit and then you're going to visit the Tombs," one of them tells her. "I think you're really going to enjoy it there."

Alex had it down perfectly. They're doing exactly what he said they would do.

I continue to look the other way so that they won't notice me, but once they're gone I walk over to where the two cells join.

"Mom," I whisper.

"Molly?" she says in total shock. "What in the world are you doing here?"

She comes over to me and we talk in whispers.

"I'm here to rescue you," I say.

"That's crazy," she tells me. "This is why I should never have let you do this. You aren't ready. It's not safe."

"You're right, it isn't safe," I say. "But I *am* ready and this is going to work. I was meant for this. Just like you. There aren't a lot of things that I'm really good at. But being an Omega, that's one that I am."

She looks at me for a moment and considers what I said. After a moment she smiles. "Okay, Molly Koala," she says. "What's the plan?"

The Great Escape

My name is Michael Bigelow and I'm here to pick up my daughter. You know, the girl who is going to be grounded for the rest of her life."

I look up from inside the holding cell and see my father in the precinct's main squad room. He's still wearing his navy-blue paramedic's uniform, and his expression is impossible to read. I can't tell if Beth has been successful in convincing him, but I'll know in a couple seconds.

"She's right over here," says Officer Strickland.

The police officer escorts him toward me, and I watch his eyes as he scans the other cells. It takes a moment before they lock on Mom. They open wide in disbelief. He can't say anything. He can't react. It will ruin the plan. He has to direct all of his anger at me, and I'm not sure he can pull it off.

"I'm really sorry, Dad," I say, my voice full of remorse. "I don't know what came over me at the zoo."

He tries to respond but he stammers, his focus still directed at Mom. He looks like he might cry.

"Are you going to be okay?" I ask.

He hesitates, but then finally answers.

"I don't know," he replies, and I have no idea if it's because of my arrest or because he sees Mom, but it's convincing. "I'm angry and I'm heartbroken and I'm trying to understand how all of this happened."

Finally he turns to look at me. "But we're a family and we are going to work this out no matter what."

I breathe a sigh of relief. That's the phrase I told Beth to give him. That's the signal that he's on board with the plan and we're ready to start.

"Well, I understand your frustration, Mr. Bigelow," says Officer Strickland. "But I get the feeling that this is a one-time only occurrence for your daughter. Isn't that right, Molly?"

"Yes, ma'am," I respond. "It will never happen again. That's a guarantee."

She unlocks the door, and I rush into my father's arms and hug him as tightly as I can. It's part of my plan, but it couldn't be more real.

"I'm so sorry, Dad," I say, looking up at his eyes, which are welling with tears. "I'm so sorry about everything."

"All I care about is that you're safe," he says. "All I care about is our family."

There's the second cue.

Suddenly my mother screams in agony and collapses to the floor. She lets out another wail and her entire body tenses up so that she's as stiff as a board.

"Are you okay?" Officer Strickland calls, jumping into action.

Mom's body begins to shake in a seizure and she starts to cough up black liquid. She's acting, but she is pulling it off with unbelievable realism.

"She's having a severe anaphylaxis episode," my dad says, breaking into paramedic lingo. "She needs to get to a hospital immediately."

It is sudden and total chaos, and Officer Strickland unlocks the door to help my mother. She bends down to assist her, but Dad stops her by grabbing her shoulder.

"Have you been inoculated against hyponeurological nanovirus?"

The police officer flashes a look of total confusion. "What?"

"Hyponeurological nanovirus? It's highly contagious and it's demonstrated by black liquid being produced by the lungs."

"No!" she says. "I haven't."

"Then do not touch her," he instructs. "I drove straight here at the end of my shift so my ambulance is in the parking lot. Let me carry her out and I'll drive her to the hospital."

Without waiting for permission Dad steps into the cell and scoops Mom up in his arms. Even in the turmoil of our little drama, I see the tender moment of connection as she slides her head onto his shoulder and he tells her, "It's going to be okay. Everything's going to be okay."

Within seconds I'm running alongside my father as he carries my mother down the long hallway toward the exit. (I told you I wouldn't be walking out the door.) I think my plan is going to work until I hear another scream from behind me.

It's one of the Dead Squad officers. He's stumbled onto the scene and sees what's happening.

"We better hurry," I say. "We've got bad guys hot on our tail."

In one swift motion my mom swings down from my father's arms like a ballroom dancer and lands on her feet in a full sprint as we rush out the door.

The ambulance is parked right by the entrance, and as we run toward it the back door flies open to reveal Beth and Grayson waiting for us. Mom and I dive in with them while Dad climbs into the driver's seat and starts the engine.

The Dead Squadder is right behind us, and he leaps onto the back bumper while I'm trying to close the door. He grabs at me and I slam the door shut, chopping off his hand so that it falls in with us.

"I think I'm going to be sick," says Beth, getting her first close-up look at zombie body parts.

"Go, go, go!" I shout, and Dad takes off across the parking lot.

Even though I've chopped off his hand, the zombie is still hanging on to the back, trying to open the door. Beth and I clamp onto the handle with all our might to keep it from opening.

"Look at that!" Grayson says, pointing out the side window.

I look up in time to see Officer Pell chasing after us along the roof of the precinct house. When he reaches the edge, he leaps into the air and lands on top of the ambulance with a huge thud.

"Keep driving!" Mom tells Dad. "Do! Not! Stop!"

She climbs up into the front passenger seat.

It the middle of all the mayhem, Dad turns to Mom as he speeds along the road.

"Last year on our anniversary," he says to her. "I swear I saw your face in the crowd."

"Outside Lincoln Center," she replies, happy at the memory.

"I knew it was you! I knew it was you!"

"You guys do realize that we have two zombies trying to beat their way into this ambulance," Beth says.

Pell's on top of the ambulance, pounding the roof, and his one-handed partner is still trying to come in the back door.

"I've got an idea," I say to Beth. "Let go of the handle."

"What?" she says as she gives me an "are you crazy?" look.

"Trust me."

We both let go at the same time and the latch opens. The zombie smiles for a second before I kick the door as hard as I can, making it fly open all the way. It knocks him off the bumper and he slams onto the street.

"Nice move!" says Beth.

I don't even have a chance to respond before Pell swings down from the roof and flings himself through the now open door like an undead gymnast. His face is contorted with rage, and he starts swinging wildly as purple spittle shoots out of his mouth.

Grayson tries to fight him but Pell slams him against the wall of the ambulance, causing medical supplies to scatter all over. He head butts Beth and knocks her down hard onto the floor.

He is completely unstoppable.

"Hello, Molly!" he hisses as he looks at me with wild eyes. His orange and yellow teeth shine bright as he reaches down and grabs me by the throat.

I gasp for air, completely unable to breathe, and flail my arms at him.

None of it matters. He just continues to tighten his grip.

My eyes start to roll back and I catch a glimpse of my mom trying to crawl back toward us to help. It doesn't seem to matter. It's too late.

I open my mouth to scream but no sound comes out, just the hiss of air escaping.

"I should have done this a long time ago!" he says, tightening his grip even more.

I start to black out, and the last image I see is his smiling face.

Then I hear an electric charge and Pell begins to convulse. It lasts about a second or two, and his eyes go wild as he tries to figure out what's happening. He has no idea, and then, without warning, his chest explodes and purple slime spews everywhere.

He just hangs there frozen in midair for a moment before his body falls dead.

As he does, he reveals Grayson, standing behind him with the electric paddles of a defibrillator in his hands. He has a look of wonder on his face, and I cannot begin to express how grateful I am that he has finally killed his first zombie.

He looks at me and I look at him, our eyes locking for a moment.

"Well, look who the hero is now," I finally manage to say.

Cain and Abel

It all started ten months ago on the first day of school. I entered the Roosevelt Island subway station wearing a necklace that once belonged to my mother. I'd worn it because it had a charm that looked like a horseshoe and I thought it might bring me luck. What I didn't know at the time is that it was actually an omega symbol, a memento of my mother's status as a zeke, or zombie killer.

A Level 3 saw it around my neck and attacked me. I was completely overmatched and survived only because

Natalie came to my rescue. Since then, whenever I return to that station, I can't help but think back to the day that changed my life forever.

I'm heading there right now, but this time everything is different. Now I'm the one looking for a fight. I'm the one planning to do the rescuing.

"All units descend on Roosevelt Island subway station, northbound platform."

That's the emergency call we hear minutes after we busted my mom out of jail and Grayson killed Officer Pell. The radio scanner in my dad's ambulance is tuned to listen in on the Dead Squad and their communications. We know they're trying to capture Milton Blackwell, and this sounds like they're getting close.

Thirty seconds later I get a call from Natalie and I put it on speaker. The reception is bad because she's in the subway station, but she's able to give us basic information about the situation.

"They've got Milton cornered on the northbound platform," she tells us. "There are three Dead Squad cops down there with him, but they're staying about ten feet away from him."

"Why aren't they just taking him?" asks Mom.

"He's got something in a vial or a test tube," she explains. "It's hard to tell exactly what it is from here, but it sure has them scared."

She explains that the Dead Squad found Milton's secret home beneath the MIST Library and chased him through a series of tunnels that ultimately led to the subway station.

"How close can you get to him?" asks my mother.

"Just to the mezzanine overlooking the platform," she replies. "They're using their status as NYPD to close down access to the stairs. We can't help him."

Before we can ask anything else, we lose the connection.

"There's no telling how long he can hold them off," says Mom. "We better get there in a hurry."

"But how can we help if they're blocking off the stairs?" I ask.

"We're not taking the stairs," Mom says. "We're taking the train."

One of the advantages of driving around in an ambulance is that you can park it almost anywhere. Minutes later we're at the Lexington Ave–63rd Street subway station, getting onto the F train. We are less than two minutes away from Roosevelt Island.

"What do you think is in the vial?" I ask my mother.

She shakes her head. "I don't know. All of his experiments are about figuring out how the Manhattan schist affects the undead."

It is so surreal to see all four members of my family together again. It's something I've dreamed about ever since we said good-bye to Mom in the hospital. Unfortunately, we don't have any time to actually be together. Mom is trying to explain some of this to Dad, but it's more than you can cover in two minutes while you're rushing to fight a zombie police force.

We're in the front car of the train, so we have a good view of the situation the moment we pull into the station.

"There they are," I say, pointing. "In the far corner."

The scene is still pretty much the same as Natalie described it. Milton is in the northernmost corner of the subway station. There are three Dead Squad cops who are blocking his way, but they're also remaining at least ten feet away. And there are more even farther back than that. Milton is disheveled, but he seems focused as he holds a vial containing a bright blue liquid.

The subway doors hiss open and the five of us step out. It's Mom, Dad, Beth, Grayson, and me. We only make it a couple of steps toward Milton before a handful of Dead Squadders come down to block our way.

"You're going to be real cool and back away," Mom instructs them. "Because Milton is going to get out of here right now."

"I'm afraid we can't let that happen."

It's Marek, and he's walking down the platform right toward us.

"I just can't seem to get you to die," he says to my mom, his voice a mixture of frustration and admiration. "I'd kill you myself, but frankly I'm not feeling my best right now."

"Clear everyone else out, Marek," Milton says the moment he sees his older brother. "This is between you and me."

"And if I don't clear them out?" Marek asks.

"Then I'll drop this and end it all."

Marek laughs and shakes his head as he continues to walk toward him. "That's the problem with baby brothers. They're always such . . . babies. Please enlighten us as to what's in your test tube?"

"It's a synthetic pathogen," he says. "The moment the liquid is exposed to air it will vaporize."

"And what will the vapor do?" Marek asks condescendingly.

"Neutralize the Manhattan schist," says Milton. "That

means it will kill the undead. Within two minutes every zombie in this room would be dead. You and me included."

This is pretty frightening. I assumed that Milton was trying to figure out how the schist kept the undead from dying in order to help them. It hadn't dawned on me that by doing so he could also counteract its power.

Unlike me, Marek isn't worried in the least. "No way," he says. "You don't have that in you. You're the lover of people, the nurturer. I'm the monster, not you."

"That all changed the moment you started to build an undead army," Milton replies. "I knew you needed to be stopped once and for all, so I built the perfect weapon for the job."

Marek is now about five feet away from Milton, and he's having trouble telling if his threat is real or not. Milton senses this hesitation and adds, "Are you willing to risk everybody's life, including your own? It's the same mistake you made when we were digging the tunnel."

This enrages Marek. "I didn't make a mistake in the tunnel! That was all you, little brother. You're the one who started all of this."

"And I'm the one who will end it."

Milton accentuates his threat by dangling the vial between his thumb and forefinger.

Marek regains his composure and turns to look at us for a moment. He locks eyes with my mother and smiles. Then he turns back to Milton.

"I don't believe for one second that you would create such a weapon, but if you did, I know you wouldn't use it here and now. It would kill your prized student right in front of her family."

"Go right ahead, Milton," says my mom. "I've been reunited with my family one last time. They know that I love them. You can drop the vial. I'm willing to be sacrificed if it means stopping him."

I see the look of devastation in my father's eyes as he clutches her hand. He's just gotten her back. He can't lose her again just moments later. Beth takes her other hand.

"It's okay," Mom reassures them.

I make eye contact with Milton, and I think he can read my panic.

"I'll do it, Marek," he replies. "I will expose everyone to *Saccharomyces cerevisiae.*"

I have to fight the urge to smile the moment I recognize the name.

The deadly pathogen is actually the harmless bacteria commonly known as yeast. I know this because every year Milton uses a vial of it as part of his first day of school lecture. He's bluffing, and the only ones that know it are my friends and family. It gives us a slight advantage.

"I do have an offer for you, though," says Milton. "Clear out all of your people, and I'll do the same. Let's just leave it to the two of us to resolve."

Marek laughs. "You want to fight? Me?"

"That's what you want, isn't it?" says Milton. "That's what you've wanted every day since that explosion."

"You mean the explosion you caused?" he replies.

"I mean the accident that did this to us, our brothers, and our cousins."

"Do you think you can fight me?" Marek asks. "Does my little scientist brother actually think he can fight big, evil Marek?"

"There's only one way to find out," says Milton.

Marek cannot resist the opportunity. He tells everyone on the Dead Squad to move back, and Milton tells us to do likewise.

Milton carefully places the vial on the ground and the two of them start to size each other up, stalking around like boxers in a ring.

"I have to be careful," says Marek. "I don't want to damage the body parts I need to have transplanted."

Milton suddenly makes a charge and throws a punch

at Marek, who simply catches the fist in his hand and stops it in midair. Then he counters with a punch that staggers Milton.

"This is just like when you were twenty," Marek says. "You think you are so much more than you actually are. Then you thought you were smart enough to build a better explosive, but you weren't. Now you think you are strong enough to fight me, but you aren't."

Marek throws another punch but Milton dodges this one and catches Marek with a punch to the jaw. Reflexively Beth, Grayson, and I let out a cheer.

"Get him, Milton!" shouts Natalie from the mezzanine.

Marek is furious and determined. "Playtime is over!"

I realize that Marek might be at his breaking point, so I step forward and march right toward the two of them.

"So this is the way the world ends," I say, reciting from the poem "The Hollow Men." "Not with a bang, but a whimper."

They both look at me in total confusion, but they stop fighting so I have my opening.

"Is there a reason you're reciting poetry?" asks Marek.

"Yes," I say. "It's from 'The Hollow Men.' Natalie says that it reminds her of you two. She says you're hollow because your life has been taken out of you. But I don't think that's why you're hollow."

I wait for either one of them to respond, but neither does, so I just keep going.

"I think you're hollow because you're missing from each other's lives," I explain, trying to think fast and keep talking. "Despite everything you've said and done, Marek, Milton is still your brother. You still love him."

He laughs derisively. "And what led you to this conclusion?"

I have now reached them, and the three of us are standing in a little triangle a few feet from each other.

"You did," I say. "That day in Central Park by the statue of Alice in Wonderland. "You said you'd like to think that your family could reunite."

Now he laughs even louder. "I was lying to you. It was a manipulation."

"That's what you tell yourself, but you weren't lying. I could see it in your eyes. It was the most honest thing I ever heard you say. It's also why you sent me those letters. Deep down there's a part of you that wanted us to figure it all out. Maybe you don't even realize it, but it's there."

He shakes his head. "You couldn't be more wrong."

"My sister and I fight," I reply. "Nothing like the two

of you. It's usually about clothes or whose turn it is to do the dishes, but we fight. And sometimes I can't stand her."

I look over at my sister and smile.

"But she's my sister and I love her more than anyone on earth."

Beth smiles back at me.

"When you were little and Milton was trampled by the horse, who rescued him? Who carried him to safety?"

I notice a change in Marek's expression. It's slight, but it's there.

"I should have left him there in the street," he says. "Then none of this would've happened."

"But you didn't leave him," I say. "Because you couldn't. He's your brother. You were heroic in his rescue. And when he became a scientist, you were proud. That's why you wanted him to make the explosive. And earlier today, that's why you named the research center at the zoo after him. He's your brother and he's a part of you."

The two of them look at each other, and I can't tell if anything I've said has made a difference.

"Could it be true?" asks Milton. "Could you still think of me as a brother?"

Marek shook his head. "Even if I could, it wouldn't matter. If I don't get your body parts, I'll be dead in a matter of days. So I guess we are going to be reunited, the two of us forming one person."

Just then there is the whoosh of a subway train as it enters the station.

"No, we won't," says Milton.

When the doors open, he surprises all of us by stepping on board.

"As soon as this train leaves the station, it will take me out of Manhattan," he says. "I will die instantly. And when I do, you will no longer be able to transplant my body parts. That means you will also die, in a matter of days."

"No!" screams Marek. "Get off the train!"

There is at most another twenty seconds before the train doors close and seal both of their fates.

"Believe it or not, I still love you," Milton says. "She's right about us always being brothers. I am forever sorry about what has happened. We should never have lived like this. We should have died in the subway tunnel all those years ago. We should have died together. Come with me. Let's leave this world as brothers and not enemies."

Milton reaches out toward him, but Marek is frozen by indecision. He does not know what to do. Then, as the train doors start to close, he leaps on board.

I look through the window right at them. They stand

face to face for a moment, and then they embrace. The last thing I see is Milton's eyes as they close and he rests his head on his brother's shoulder.

A rush of air roars out of the station as the F train departs and disappears into the darkened tunnel that leads to Queens. Moments later it passes beyond the protective blanket of the Manhattan schist.

Marek and Milton Blackwell are dead.

Ωmega

My family will never be . . . *normal.* That was true even before the undead disrupted our lives. But now, we'll be even less normal than before. It's been an odd couple of weeks since that day we broke Mom out of jail and watched Milton and Marek ride off in the subway.

Don't get me wrong; it's great that the four of us are together. But there are still a lot of adjustments that have to be made. After all, my mom is undead, and even though there isn't an evil dark lord of the underworld trying to kill her, there will be some complications. My dad thought he had buried her forever, but he never stopped loving her. That's the key to all of it . . . love. If you love someone, nothing else really matters.

My family is everything to me, and when I use that word I don't just mean the people who share the same blood that I do. (In fact, some of them don't even have blood.) No, I use it to mean the people who share my heart. All the people I love.

We are gathered together at the moment because this is family night. Well, technically it's family day, and the rules are both simple and ironclad. When it's my turn to pick what we do, then you have to do what I say. That's why all of us are out on the Great Lawn in Central Park.

We had to spread out three blankets just to hold all the food that Dad made for the picnic. Alex is devouring fried chicken at a record pace while he talks to Beth about the play she's directing at drama camp. Grayson and Liberty are locked in an epic match of One Foot Trivia as Natalie does everything she can to come up with questions to stump them. And my parents are holding hands, laughing at each other's stories and listening to *La Traviata*.

In other words, even though it's not normal, it's still pretty close to perfect.

I close my eyes and turn my face toward the sun so that

its warmth radiates through my body. I inhale the delicious aromas of food and fresh air, and I listen to the music of people laughing and having fun.

I'm wearing my mother's necklace, the one that started me on this adventure, and I reach up and press the omega symbol between my thumb and finger.

Omega is the last letter of the Greek alphabet, and it's often used to signify the end of something. It was chosen as the name of our secret society because we were to be the last word on the undead. But omega is also the first letter of the Greek word for family. So, in that way, what is an ending is also a beginning.

I open my eyes and look at my family and know that I am the person I am supposed to be. I think back to when we used to come here and my mom would read *Alice's Adventures in Wonderland* to us. I remember her favorite line from the book: *It's no use going back to yesterday, because I was a different person then.*

It really is no use going back, and I have no interest in doing so.

My name is Molly Bigelow, and I am ready for whatever comes next.

Acknowledgments

I am forever indebted to the people who have helped bring the Dead City books to life. It is a debt that I will try to repay with everything from cupcakes to friendship. First on the list are the amazing people at Simon & Schuster. There is the dynamic duo of Fiona Simpson and Mara Anastas, and their Omega team of Nigel Quarless, Kayley Hoffman, Jessica Handelman, Karina Granda, Kara Reilly, Emma Sector, Carolyn Swerdloff, Teresa Ronquillo, Michelle Leo, Candace Green, Anthony Parisi, Kelsey Dickinson, Sara Jane Abbott, and the remarkable Lauren Forte. (Go Mets!)

Those of you who think Molly Bigelow is too good to be true have obviously never met my agent, Rosemary Stimola. Like Molly, ro stimo is straight out of Queens and possesses the perfect blend of tough and tender, brilliant and brave. I'm just glad she decided to rep authors instead of fighting zombies. (Although I wouldn't be surprised if she does that on the side.)

I also want to thank the people who take the time to read the books and share them. They are teachers, librarians, and readers like Brady, Bayla, and Peyton, who stay up late at night because they just have to know what happens next. You are my rock stars.

And finally there is my family, who makes everything possible. They inspire and encourage. They read and edit. They live and breathe on every page. The love that exists between the characters in the books is a reflection of the love they give me every day.

Ωmega Today! Ωmega Forever!